Helen Bianchin

THE HUSBAND TEST

Passion™

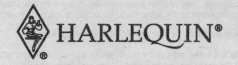

HARLEQUIN®

TORONTO • NEW YORK • LONDON
AMSTERDAM • PARIS • SYDNEY • HAMBURG
STOCKHOLM • ATHENS • TOKYO • MILAN • MADRID
PRAGUE • WARSAW • BUDAPEST • AUCKLAND

ISBN 0-373-12218-7

THE HUSBAND TEST

First North American Publication 2001.

CHAPTER ONE

KATRINA felt her breath hitch a little as her voice rose in disbelief. 'You're not serious?'

It was a joke. A tasteless, sick joke. Except lawyers didn't sink to this level of facetiousness during a professional consultation. 'Dear God,' she said irreverently. 'You *are* serious.'

The man seated behind the imposing mahogany desk shifted his shoulders, and eased into a well-rehearsed platitude. 'Your late father expressed concern at the difficulties you might incur.'

Difficulties didn't even begin to describe the shenanigans her extended dysfunctional family were heaping on her head.

Not that this was anything new. She had been *the favoured one* for as long as she could remember. Daddy's golden girl. His only child. A constant, immovable thorn in the side of his second and third wives and their child apiece from previous marriages.

No one could say her life hadn't been interesting, Katrina reflected. Three paternal divorces, two scheming ex-wives, and two equally devious stepsiblings.

During her formative years she'd been able to escape to boarding school. Except for holidays at home, most of which had been hell on wheels as she'd fought a battle in an ongoing war where reality had been a seething sea of emotional and mental one-upmanship beneath the façade of pleasant inter-family relationships.

The time between each of her father's divorces had proved to be the lull before the next storm, and instead of bowing her down it had merely strengthened her desire to be a worthy successor to his extensive business interests.

Much to the delight of the man who'd sired her.

Now, that same man was intent on reaching out a hand from the grave to resurrect a part of her life she fought on a daily basis to forget.

Katrina cast the lawyer a penetrating look. 'He can't do this,' she refuted firmly as she attempted to hide the faint tide of panic that was slowly invading her body.

'Your father had your best interests at heart.'

'Making the terms of his will conditional on me effecting a reconciliation with my ex-husband?' she queried scathingly. It was ridiculous!

'I understand a divorce has not been formalised.'

Her level of desperation moved up a notch. She hadn't got around to it and, as no papers had been served on her, neither had Nicos.

'I have no intention of allowing Nicos Kasoulis back into my life.'

Greek-born, Nicos had emigrated to Australia at a young age with his parents. As a young adult he'd gained various degrees, then had entered the hi-tech industry, inheriting his father's extensive business interests when both parents died in an aircraft crash.

Katrina had met him at a party, their instant attraction mutual, and they'd married three months later.

'Kevin appointed Nicos Kasoulis an executor,' the lawyer relayed. 'Shortly before his death, your father also appointed him to the board of directors of Macbride.'

Why hadn't she been apprised of that? Dammit, she held a responsible position in the Macbride conglomerate. Choosing not to take her into his confidence was paternal manipulation at its worst.

Her chin lifted fractionally. 'I shall contest the will.' Dammit, he couldn't do this to her!

'The conditions are iron-clad,' the lawyer reiterated gently. 'Each of your father's ex-wives will receive a specified lump sum plus an annuity until such time as they remarry, sufficient to support a reasonable lifestyle in the principal residence they gained at the time of their divorce. There are a few bequests to charity, but the remainder of the estate passes in equal one-third shares to you and Nicos, with the remaining share being held in trust for your children. There is a stipulation,' he continued, 'making it conditional both you and Nicos Kasoulis refrain from filing for divorce, and reside in the same residence together for the minimum term of one year.'

Had Nicos Kasoulis known of these conditions when he'd attended her father's funeral less than a week ago?

Without doubt, Katrina decided grimly, recalling how he'd stood like a dark angel on the fringes, watchful, his touch cool, almost impersonal, as he'd taken her hand in his and had brushed his lips to her cheek.

He'd uttered a few words in condolence, politely declined to attend the wake held in Kevin Macbride's home, and had walked to his car, slid in behind the wheel, and driven away.

'And if I choose not to heed my late father's request?'

'Nicos Kasoulis retains control in the boardroom, and a financial interest in Macbride.'

She didn't believe him, *couldn't* accept Kevin had gone to such lengths to satisfy a whim to have his daughter reconcile with a man he had considered more than her equal.

'That's ridiculous,' Katrina refuted. *She* was the rightful heir to the Macbride business empire. Dammit, it wasn't about money...nor bricks and mortar, stocks and bonds.

It was what they represented. The sweat and toil of a young Irish lad from Tullamore who at the age of fifteen had worked his way to Australia to begin a new life in Sydney as a brickie's labourer. At twenty-one he'd formed his own company and made his first million. At thirty he'd become a legend, and had been fêted as such. With the pick of Sydney's society maidens to choose from, he'd acquired a wife, sired a babe, and had developed a roving eye. Something that had got him into trouble and out of marriage a few too many times. A lovable rogue, as Katrina's mother had referred to Kevin Macbride on a good day.

To Katrina he'd been a saint. A tall dark-haired man whose laugh had begun in his belly and had rolled out into the air as a full-blooded shout. Someone who'd swept her up into his arms, rubbed his sun-drenched cheek against her own fair one, told stories that would have charmed the fairies, and who'd loved her unconditionally.

From a young age she'd played pretend Monopoly with his kingdom, sitting on his knee, absorbing every business fact he'd imparted. During school holidays she'd accompanied him to building sites, had had her own hard hat, and had been able to cuss as well as any hardened labourer—mentally. For if Kevin had caught even a whisper of such language falling from her lips he'd never have allowed her on *any* site again.

Something that would have hurt far more than a paternal slap, for she'd inherited his love of creating something magnificent from bricks and mortar. Of siting the land, envisaging architectural design, selecting the materials, the glass, seeing it rise from the ground to finish as a masterpiece. Houses, buildings, office towers. In later years Kevin Macbride had delegated, but everything that bore his stamp had received his personal touch. It had been his Irish pride, and her own, to see that it was done.

To imagine conceding *any* of it to Nicos Kasoulis was unconscionable. She couldn't, *wouldn't* do it. Macbride belonged to a Macbride.

'You refuse?'

The lawyer's smooth tones intruded, and she lifted

her chin in a gesture of defiance. 'Nicos Kasoulis will not gain sole control of Macbride.'

Her eyes were the green of the fields of her father's homeland. Brilliant, lush. Emphasised by the pale cream texture of her skin, the deep auburn hair that fell in a river of dark red-gold silky curls down her back.

For all that Kevin Macbride had been a big man, his only child had inherited her mother's petite frame and slender curves, the hair and eyes from her paternal grandmother, and a temper to match.

Too much woman for many a man, the lawyer mused, who'd long been intrigued by the private life of one of the city's icons whose business interests had commanded large legal fees over the years.

'You will, therefore, adhere to your father's wishes as set out in his will?'

Live with Nicos Kasoulis? Share a home, her life, with him for one year? 'If that's what it takes,' Katrina vowed solemnly, and he was willing to swear he caught a hint of tensile steel that boded ill for any man hoping to bend her will.

Was Nicos Kasoulis that man? He would have thought so, given the look of him. Yet, despite the marriage, they'd separated after a few brief months, and rumour rarely held much basis for fact.

His business was to ensure Kevin Macbride's wishes were legally maintained. Not to wonder at the man's private life, nor that of his only child.

'I shall despatch formal notification of your willingness to comply.'

Katrina lifted one eyebrow, and her voice was dry and totally lacking in humour. 'Did my father specify a date for this reconciliation?'

'Within seven days of his passing.'

Kevin Macbride had never been one to waste time, but a week was over-zealous, surely?

She looked around the sumptuous furnishings, the expensive prints adorning the walls, the heavy plate-glass and caught the view out over the harbour.

Suddenly she wanted out of here, away from officialdom and legalities. She needed to feel the fresh air on her face, to put the top down on her Porsche and drive, let the breeze toss her hair and bring colour to her cheeks. To be free to think, before she had to deal with Nicos.

With determined resolve she rose to her feet. 'I imagine we'll be in touch again before long.' There would be documents to sign, the due process of winding up a deceased's estate. She extended her hand in a formal gesture that concluded the appointment, murmured a few polite words in parting, then she moved into the corridor leading to Reception.

The lawyer walked at her side, then stood as she passed through the double glass doors and stepped towards the lift.

There was no doubt Katrina Kasoulis was a beautiful young woman. Something about the way she held herself, her grace of movement, and that hair...

He hid a faint sigh, for she burned as a bright flame, and a man could get singed just from looking.

Katrina rode the lift down to the ground floor,

crossed the street to the adjacent car park, located the relevant floor, and slid in behind the wheel of her car.

It was almost five, the day's office hours reaching a close, and she eased the Porsche onto street level, then entered the stream of city traffic.

Katrina drove, negotiating the choked roadways until she'd covered distance and the traffic dissipated. Then she moved into a higher gear, heard the muted response of the finely tuned engine, and revelled in the speed.

It was almost six when she pulled to a halt on the grassy bank overlooking the beach. There was a tanker on the horizon, easing slowly down towards the inner harbour, and a few children frolicked in the shallows beneath the watchful eye of their parents.

Gulls crested low over the water, dipped, skidded along the surface and settled, only to move their wings in a graceful arc to skim onto the sand.

It was a peaceful scene, one she desperately needed to ease the ache of recent loss. There had been so much to organise, family to deal with.

And now there was Nicos.

It was over, done with. And she'd healed.

Liar.

She only had to think of him to remember how it had been between them. Not a day went past that her subconscious didn't force a memory. He invaded her mind, possessed her dreams, and became her worst nightmare.

All too frequently she woke in a sweat, his hands,

his mouth on her so real she could almost swear he'd been there with her.

Yet she'd always be alone, the security system intact, and she'd spend what remained of the night reading or watching a late movie on television in an attempt to dispel his haunting image.

Occasionally she bumped into him at social gatherings around the city, professional soirées where her presence was *de rigueur*. Then they greeted each other, exchanged polite conversation...and moved on. Except she was acutely conscious of him, his steady gaze, the latent power he exuded, and his sensual heat.

Even now her pulse quickened to a faster beat, and her skin warmed, the soft body hairs raising in awareness. Sensation unfurled deep inside, and spread through her body like a lick of flame, activating each pleasure pulse, every erotic zone.

This was crazy. She took a deep, steadying breath and held onto it, then slowly exhaled. Two, three times over.

Focus, she bade silently. Remember *why* you walked out on him.

Dear Lord, how could she *forget* Nicos's ex-mistress relaying news of a confirmed pregnancy and naming Nicos as the father of her unborn child?

Georgia Burton, a model whose slender beauty graced several magazine covers, had delighted in informing a conception date coinciding with a time when Nicos had been out of town on business.

Georgia's assurance her affair with Nicos hadn't

ended with his marriage was something Katrina couldn't condone, despite Nicos's adamant denial, and after one argument too many she'd simply packed up her things and moved into temporary accommodation.

Even now, several months later, the memory, the pain, was just as intense as it had been the day she had left him.

The peal of her cell phone sounded loud in the silence, interrupting the solitude, and she checked the caller ID, saw it was her mother, and took the call.

'Siobhan?'

'Darling, have you forgotten you're joining me for dinner and the theatre tonight?'

Katrina closed her eyes and stifled a curse. 'Can we skip dinner? I'll collect you at seven-thirty.' She could just about make it if she edged over the speed limit, took the quickest shower on record, and dressed.

'Seven forty-five. I have tickets, and valet parking will eliminate several minutes.'

She made it...just. Together they entered the auditorium and slid into their seats just as the curtain rose.

Katrina focussed on the stage, the actors, and blocked out everything else. It was a technique she'd learned at a young age, and now it served her well.

Between acts she gathered with her mother among patrons in the lobby, sipped a cool drink, and indulged in conversation. Siobhan owned a boutique in exclusive Double Bay, and had in the years since her divorce become an astute and extremely successful businesswoman.

'I've put something aside for you,' Siobhan relayed.

Her mother's taste in clothes was impeccable, and Katrina proffered a warm smile. 'Thanks. I'll write you a cheque.'

Siobhan pressed her hand on that of her daughter. 'A gift, darling.'

A prickle of awareness slithered down Katrina's spine, and she barely caught herself from shivering in reaction.

Only one man had this effect on her, and she turned slowly, forcing herself to skim the fellow patrons with casual interest.

A difficult feat when all her body's self-protective instincts were on full alert.

Nicos Kasoulis stood as part of a group, his head inclined towards a gorgeous blonde whose avid attention was almost sickening. Two men, two women. A cosy foursome.

Yet even as she was about to turn away he lifted his head and captured her glance, held it, those dark eyes steady, mesmeric, almost frightening.

He had the height, Katrina conceded, the breadth of shoulder, the stance, that drew attention.

Sculptured facial bone structure inherited from his Greek ancestors—wide cheekbones, strong jaw, not to mention a mouth that promised a thousand sensual delights and eyes as dark as sin—merely added another dimension to a man who wore an aura of power as comfortably as a second skin. Thick dark hair worn longer than was currently conventional added an individualistic tone to a man whose strength of will was equally admired as well as feared among his contemporaries.

If he thought to intimidate her, he was mistaken. Katrina lifted her chin, and her eyes flashed with green fire an instant before she deliberately turned her back on him.

At that moment the electronic buzzer sounded, heralding patrons to return to their seats.

Katrina's focus was shot to hell, and the final act passed in a blur of dialogue and action that held little consequence. Her entire train of thought was centred around escaping the auditorium without bumping into the man who'd stirred her to passionate heights, the mere thought of which caused her equilibrium to crash and burn.

An escape Nicos would contrive to allow, or not, as the mood took him.

Not, she perceived as they made their way through the lobby to the front entrance.

'Katrina. Siobhan.'

His voice was like black satin, dark and smoothly dangerous beneath the veneer of sophisticated politeness.

'Why, Nicos,' her mother breathed with delight as he bent to brush his lips to her cheek. 'How nice to see you.'

Traitor, Katrina accorded silently. Siobhan had

been one of Nicos's conquests from the beginning. Still was.

'Likewise.' He turned slightly and fixed Katrina with a deceptively mild gaze. 'Dinner tomorrow night. Seven?'

Bastard. The curse stopped in her throat as she caught her mother's surprise. Nicos, damn him, merely arched an eyebrow.

'Katrina hasn't told you?'

She wanted to hit him, and almost did. 'No.' The single word escaped as a furious negative.

Siobhan looked from her daughter to Nicos, who merely inclined his head in silent deference to Katrina.

Grr! She wanted to scratch his eyes out, and for a wild nanosecond she actually considered it.

He knew, darn it. She could tell from the faint musing gleam evident, the slight quirk at the edge of his mouth as he waited for her to pick up the ball and play.

There was no way around it, and better the truth than prevarication. 'Kevin, in his infinite wisdom,' she declared with heavy irony, 'has made it a condition of his will that I reside in the same house with Nicos for a year. If I don't, Nicos gains a majority control of Macbride.' She threw him a dark look that would have felled a lesser man. 'Something I absolutely refuse to let happen.'

'Oh, my,' Siobhan voiced faintly, her eyes clouding as she glimpsed her daughter's simmering temper.

Siobhan knew her ex-husband well. The iron will

beneath the soft, persuasive Irish charm. It had been a time ago, and she'd long forgiven him. For the one good thing to come out of their union had been Katrina.

'The man's a meddling fool,' she said quietly, and saw her daughter's wry smile. But a smart one. Oh, yes, Kevin Macbride had been nothing if not astute. And he'd developed an instant liking for the attractive Greek his daughter had wed. Maybe, just maybe, the father might achieve in death what he hadn't been able to achieve while he'd been alive.

Siobhan, how could you? Katrina seethed silently. While I'm capable of slaying my own dragons, I expected you to stand beside me, not welcome the enemy with grace and charm.

Nicos discerned each and every fleeting expression on his wife's features. She'd lost weight, her skin was pale, and at the moment she was a seething bundle of barely controlled fury. A bundle he was hard-pressed not to heft over one shoulder and carry kicking and cursing out to his car. And ultimately into his bed.

Katrina glimpsed the intent in those dark eyes, and wanted to *hit* him. 'Goodnight.'

The word was evinced as a cool dismissal. Icy, with a tinge of disdain meant to convey the edge of her temper.

She saw what he was going to do an instant before his head descended, and he anticipated her move, countered it, and captured her mouth with his own in a kiss that destroyed her carefully erected defences.

Brief, possessive, evocative, it brought a vivid reminder of what had been.

And would be again.

The purpose was there, a silent statement that was neither threat nor challenge. Merely fact.

Then he straightened, and his lips curved into a musing smile as he caught the unmistakable edge of anger in her glittering green gaze.

'Seven, Katrina,' he reminded her with deceptive quietness, and saw her chin tilt fractionally.

Cool, control. She'd had plenty of practice at displaying both emotions. 'Name the restaurant, and I'll meet you there.'

One eyebrow arched. A silent, faintly mocking gesture that put a serious dent in her bid for independence.

'The foyer of the Ritz-Carlton.'

An established, élite hotel situated a few blocks from her Double Bay apartment, negating the need to take her car.

She had no doubt it was a deliberate choice on his part, and she was sorely tempted to stamp her foot in childish repudiation. Instead, she offered him a cool glance and kept her voice neutral. 'Fine.'

Nicos inclined his head towards Siobhan, then he turned and began weaving his way through numerous patrons converging near the entrance.

'Don't say a word,' Katrina warned in caution as they gained the external pavement.

'Darling, I wouldn't dream of it,' her mother evinced with a soft chuckle.

CHAPTER TWO

THE evening was warm, the air like silk on a soft breeze whispering in from the sea as Katrina locked her car and set the alarm.

The hotel entrance lay ahead, its elegant façade attesting élite patronage in an established, moneyed inner-city suburb.

She'd dressed to kill, although only she knew how much time had been spent selecting and discarding one set of clothes after another in a quest to do battle and win.

Nicos viewed her entry into the lounge with veiled interest.

Business, he silently attested, noting the power suit in stylish black. The cut of the jacket, the mid-thigh length of the straight skirt, the sheer black hose showcasing shapely legs, slim ankles emphasised by stiletto-heeled black pumps. Jewellery confined to a diamond pendant on a slender gold chain, and a simple diamond stud worn in each earlobe.

Was she aware how well he could read her? The tiny signals that indicated her mood were evident in the sweep of her hair into a smooth, sophisticated French twist, the perfectly applied make-up, highlighting her eyes, the shape of her mouth. The tilt of her chin.

It was a façade, one he'd been able to dispense with easily. He retained a vivid memory of the way she melted beneath his touch. The spill of hair as he slid his fingers through its thick length and cupped her nape, angling her head so that soft, evocative mouth lifted to meet his own. The wild, untamed passion of her response as she met and matched him, treading a path to mutual satisfaction that was more, much more than he'd shared with any other woman in his lifetime.

He saw the moment she sighted him, and glimpsed the faint straightening of her shoulders, the way her fingers tightened over her evening purse. Her step didn't falter as she crossed towards him.

'Nicos.' Her greeting was polite, almost cool.

Take control, a tiny voice prompted. 'Shall we go through?'

Fire and ice, he mused. A combination that never failed to intrigue him. 'Eager to be done, Katrina?'

Her gaze met and held his. 'I'd prefer to keep this short,' she stated civilly, and caught the imperceptible lift of those broad shoulders.

'Such honesty,' he chided softly.

He made no attempt to touch her, but this close she was all too aware of his body heat, the faint tang of his exclusive cologne. Not to mention the aura of leashed power that was so much a part of him.

He was biding his time, she alluded with a tinge of bitterness. Tonight was a mere indulgence. A social formality in an attempt to create some form of mutual truce whereby they could co-exist for the next year.

Nicos had nothing to lose, while *she*...

Don't think about it, she chided silently as she entered the restaurant at Nicos's side.

Seated, she let him choose the wine while she perused the menu, ordering after scant deliberation a starter and a side salad.

'Not hungry?' Nicos posed as he watched her sip the excellent Chardonnay.

Katrina met his gaze with equanimity. 'Not particularly.' Her stomach felt as if it were attempting intricate somersaults, and the movement was not conducive to the easy digestion of food.

It irked that he could still have this effect. Worse, that all it took was one look at him and her pulse raced to a faster beat.

Was he aware of it? She hoped not. She'd spent a lifetime learning to mask her feelings. To smile, and pretend she was immune from the barbs two stepmothers and two stepsiblings had inflicted at every opportunity.

Adopting a façade wasn't difficult. She did it every day of her life. Professionally. Emotionally.

'Let's get this over with, shall we?'

'Why not finish your meal first?' Nicos countered silkily.

Katrina picked at her salad, then discarded it. 'I've lost my appetite.'

'Some more wine?'

'No. Thanks,' she added politely. The need for a clear head was essential.

Dammit, why did he have to be so blatantly male?

He savoured his food as he savoured a woman. With care, enjoyment, and satisfaction.

There was something incredibly sensual about the movement of his hands, and she had only to look at his mouth to imagine how it felt on her own. The devastation it could wreak as he pleasured her. He had the touch, the knowledge, to drive a woman wild.

Focus, she chided silently. This isn't about you. Or Nicos. It's about claiming a right to Macbride.

'We need to decide whose residence we'll share,' she began firmly.

He forked a succulent piece of fish, and followed it with a portion of salad. 'Naturally you'd prefer your apartment.'

It couldn't be this easy. 'Yes.'

He cast her a measured look. 'The Point Piper house is large. It would be more convenient for you to move in there.'

It surprised her that he hadn't sold the luxurious mansion they'd occupied for the few brief months of their ill-fated marriage. An architectural masterpiece built against sloping rock-face, it encompassed three levels of modern living, with terraced grounds, ornamental gardens, a swimming pool, and a magnificent harbour view.

It also housed too many memories. 'No, it wouldn't.'

Nicos replaced his cutlery and settled back comfortably in his chair. 'Afraid, Katrina?'

She looked at him carefully, noting his steady gaze, the seemingly relaxed expression. Deceptive to the unwary, she acknowledged silently, for Nicos Kasoulis possessed a razor-sharp mind and a killer instinct. Qualities that had gained him immense respect from both friend and foe. In the business arena, and among the socially élite.

It had been this ruthless streak that had appealed so much to Kevin Macbride, who'd seen in Nicos what he'd himself possessed: someone who knew what he wanted and went after it regardless of anything or anyone who stood in his way.

'Have I reason to be?'

His smile held a certain wryness. 'You must know I have your welfare at heart.'

'If that were so, you'd have stood down as executor of Kevin's will.'

'I gave him my word.'

'And that is everything.'

'Cynicism doesn't suit you.'

Katrina picked up her glass, and took a leisurely sip of wine. 'Forgive me,' she said without any hint of apology. 'I learned it at any early age.'

'Why not try a dessert?' Nicos queried blandly, and saw the fire bank beneath those brilliant green eyes.

She took a deep breath and sought to retain a semblance of calm. 'We need to arrive at some sort of compromise.'

Nicos slid a hand into the inside pocket of his jacket, extracted a bulky envelope, and tossed it down onto the table in front of her.

Katrina viewed it with suspicion. 'What's this?'

'A remote for the front gates, and keys to my home.'

He was far too sure of himself. 'Presumptuous, aren't you?'

'Practical,' he corrected.

'Arrogant,' she attested. 'What if I insist you move into my apartment?' she queried heatedly, hating him at that moment.

'Do you really want me in the next bedroom to yours?' Nicos queried mildly. 'Sharing the same living quarters, the same kitchen? In an apartment more suited to one person than two?'

'You know nothing about my apartment,' she retaliated, and saw the slight lift of his eyebrow.

'I was responsible for the gutting and rebuilding of the original homestead.'

She cast him a scathing look. 'Next you'll tell me you own it.'

Nicos inclined his head. 'Guilty.'

If she'd known, she'd never have bought it. Her eyes narrowed. Come to think of it, it had been her father who'd first drawn her attention to the penthouse apartment in the large, modernised, tri-level home. Less than a month after she'd walked out on Nicos.

Nicos watched the fleeting emotions chase across her expressive features before she successfully masked them.

'Mythos Investments is one of my companies.'

Of course. The name alone should have alerted her, but at the time she hadn't given much thought to anything other than finding a solitary haven of her own.

Suspicion ignited, and demanded answer. 'Did you employ a private detective to monitor my every move?' Katrina queried tightly.

An ex-military whose instructions were to observe, protect if necessary, and be unobtrusive at all times. A successful operation, Nicos acknowledged, for which the man had received a handsome remuneration.

His silence was more eloquent than mere words, and Katrina's mouth thinned. 'I see.'

Nicos's gaze speared hers. 'What do you see, *pedhi mou*?' His voice was dangerously quiet.

Too quiet. Like the calm before a storm. Something she chose to ignore.

'Two men bent on manipulating my life,' she retaliated fiercely. 'My father during his lifetime, and now *you*.' She picked up her water glass and momentarily toyed with the idea of throwing its contents in his face.

'Don't,' Nicos warned softly.

She was caught on the brink of violence. Aware of the acute satisfaction of such an action, and the folly of carrying it through. 'You read minds?'

'Yours.'

She took in a deep breath and released it slowly. 'The activity reports would have been incredibly repetitive,' she began tightly.

Work, social activities. A few male partners, none of whom had stayed overnight.

'How *dare* you?' The anger bubbled over. 'It was

an invasion of privacy. Harassment. I should file charges against you!'

His gaze didn't waver. 'It was protection.'

'Did Kevin know?' she demanded starkly.

'We discussed it.'

Traitors, both of them. 'Dear heaven,' she breathed with pious disregard. 'I'm twenty-seven, not seventeen!'

'You're the daughter of a very wealthy man, and—'

'The estranged wife of someone who is almost my father's equal,' Katrina finished bitterly.

'Yes.'

'I hate you.'

His shoulders lifted in an imperturbable shrug. 'So—hate me. At least it's an active emotion.'

She was steaming, her anger a palpable entity.

He caught the way her fingers curled into her palm, the whiteness of her knuckles as she sought control.

'If you leave now, you'll only delay the inevitable,' Nicos warned silkily. 'And invoke a repeat performance.'

It didn't help that he was right.

'I don't want this,' she vowed with unaccustomed vehemence. 'Any of it.'

'But you want Macbride.'

It was a statement she didn't, *couldn't* refute.

Why should sharing a residence for a year with her estranged husband pose any problems? They were both adults. They had extensive work obligations, separate interests. With luck, they'd hardly see each other much at all.

A tiny bubble of laughter rose and died in her throat. Who was she kidding?

Katrina looked at the bulky envelope, then lifted her head and met his enigmatic gaze. 'I won't share a bedroom with you.'

Their eyes clashed, brilliant green and dark brown. And held. She wasn't conscious of the way her breath hitched, or its slow release several long seconds later.

'I don't believe I asked you to.'

His voice was cool, almost ice, and she contained a slight shiver as it threatened to slither the length of her spine.

'Friday,' Katrina stated. The seventh day, thus fulfilling the first condition listed in Kevin's will. 'Evening,' she qualified.

'I won't be home until late.'

One eyebrow arched in disdain. 'I don't see that as a problem.'

Nicos inclined his head, signalled the waiter, and ordered coffee.

'Not for me.' She had to get out of here, away from the man who'd once held her heart, her world, in his hands.

Whatever needed to be faced, she'd face on Friday. But for now, she wanted to be as far away from Nicos Kasoulis as possible.

With unhurried movements she rose to her feet, collected her evening purse, barely stifling a startled gasp as Nicos unfolded his lengthy frame and caught hold of her wrist.

'What do you think you're doing?' she vented with an angry snap.

'I'd say it's obvious.'

The waiter appeared out of nowhere, accepted the cash Nicos handed him, beamed appreciatively at the size of the tip, and Katrina had little option but to allow Nicos to accompany her from the restaurant.

The instant they reached the foyer she tried to wrench her hand from his, and failed miserably. Short of an undignified struggle she was compelled to walk at his side through the elegant arcade to the street.

'If you don't let my hand go, I'll scream,' she threatened, *sotto voce.*

'Go ahead,' Nicos directed imperturbably. 'I imagine female histrionics will garner some attention.'

'You're the most impossible man I've ever met!'

His quiet laughter was the living end.

'Go to hell!'

'You don't want me to take you there,' Nicos warned with a dangerous silkiness that sent ice slithering down the length of her spine.

'I don't want you...*finis.*'

'Is that a challenge?'

'A statement.'

'A year, Katrina. Maybe we could attempt a truce of sorts?'

She spared him an angry glance. 'I doubt it's possible.'

'Try,' he suggested succinctly.

She reached into her evening purse, extracted a set of keys, and indicated the sleek white Porsche parked kerbside. 'My car.'

'Proving a point, Katrina?'

'Yes.'

'Perhaps I should follow your example.' He lowered his head and pulled her close in one easy movement.

She opened her mouth to protest, but no word escaped as he took possession in a manner that reached right down to her soul. And tugged at something long dormant. Evoking a vivid memory of how it used to be between them.

Of its own accord her body sank in against his, savouring for a brief few seconds the feeling of coming home. Of recognition at the most base level, and need.

The slow sweep of his tongue explored her own, tangled, then took her deep.

Dear Lord, how could she be this needy?

With a reluctant groan she tore her mouth away, and attempted to put some distance between them. Her own distress was evident, and she fought a mixture of anger and resentment as he brushed his knuckles along the edge of her jaw.

'Chemistry,' she dismissed with practised flippancy.

His eyes were dark, his expression unreadable, and she stifled a silent curse.

'You think so?' He took the keys from her hand,

deactivated the alarm, then he unlocked the door. He opened it, slid the key into the ignition, then stood to one side as she slipped in behind the wheel.

'Friday, Katrina.'

As if she needed reminding. With a deft twist of the wrist she gunned the engine into life, eased out of the parking space, then she sent the car forward at a quick pace.

She barely had time to shift through the gears before it was necessary to change down as she reached the driveway to her apartment.

Minutes later she'd garaged the Porsche and was safely indoors, choosing the lift instead of stairs to reach her apartment.

It wasn't late, only a few minutes past nine. Too early to go to bed. She toyed with the idea of phoning any one of several friends, suggesting she meet up with them and share a drink and chat a while. Except they would ask questions at such an impulsive action, and questions were something she'd prefer to avoid.

Instead, she undressed, pulled on an oversized tee shirt, removed her make-up, then she curled up in a comfortable armchair and changed channels on the television until she found something worth watching.

Katrina must have fallen asleep, for when she woke her neck felt stiff, one leg was numb, and a glance at her watch revealed it was long past midnight.

Minutes later she doused the lights and crawled into bed to lie awake haunted by the feel of Nicos's mouth on her own.

*   *   *

Choosing what to pack required minimum effort. A selection of clothes for the office, casual gear, and a few suitable outfits for the rare social occasion.

Katrina closed the zip on both suitcases, took one last look around the apartment, then she set the security alarm, closed the outer door, and summoned the lift down to the basement garage.

It was only a few kilometres from Double Bay to Point Piper, and no matter how she qualified the move it was impossible to control her nervous tension as she turned into the elegant street housing Nicos's home.

Katrina eased the car to a halt, engaged the remote control, waited as the high wrought-iron gate slid smoothly to one side, then she traversed the semi-circular driveway towards a stylish tri-level home set in well-kept grounds. One of many in this tree-lined street where a mix of old and new residences provided an air of wealth in a harbour-front suburb.

The wide portico framed an impressive entry with ornate double doors protected by a sophisticated security system.

A married couple came in each weekday to clean and tend the grounds, but they would have left hours ago, Katrina reflected as she entered the lobby.

The house was silent, and it was impossible to shrug off a sense of *déjà vu*.

Late-afternoon sun hit the ornamental multi-paned leaded glass, sending prisms of soft pinks and greens across the cream marble-tiled floor, showcasing the high ceilings, the wide curved staircase leading to an oval balcony, an elegant chandelier.

To her right lay a large formal lounge and dining room, to her left a study, an informal sitting room, dining room and kitchen.

A spacious entertainment room, sauna, spa, gym, were situated on the lower floor, together with an indoor swimming pool with wide French doors leading out onto terraced gardens.

Five bedrooms, each with *en suite*, comprised the upper level of a beautifully furnished house with magnificent views out over the inner harbour.

For a brief few months it had been *home*. A place where she'd shared love, laughter, and great passion.

Don't go there, a tiny voice warned.

Discipline was something she'd mastered at a young age, yet she was helpless against the unwanted emotions invading her mind, her body.

Re-entering Nicos Kasoulis's space was a move fraught with tension. Yet what choice did she have?

None, if she wanted control of Macbride, Katrina reflected a trifle pensively as she ascended stairs to the upper floor.

Did Nicos occupy the master suite they'd once shared? Or had he moved into one of the other bedrooms?

The master suite, she determined minutes later. His clothes were there, and an array of masculine toiletries took up space on the marbled vanity.

She skimmed a glance over the large bed, and endeavoured to still her increased heartbeat. How could he bear to stay here? Occupy this room, this *bed*?

Pain clenched in her stomach, and she turned

abruptly away in an attempt to stifle a host of memories.

Control, she had it. But for how long? a devilish imp taunted as she chose a bedroom on the opposite side of the balcony.

There was, she saw at once, a small desk ideal for her laptop. A calculated guess on Nicos's part that she'd select this room, or sheer coincidence?

Second-guessing Nicos's motivation was a fruitless exercise.

Move your gear in, unpack, take a shower, check your e-mails, make a few calls, then have an early night, she prompted silently.

It was almost ten when hunger forced the realisation she'd missed dinner. Lunch had been a sandwich eaten at her desk, and breakfast had comprised orange juice and black coffee.

Hardly adequate sustenance, she decided as she made her way down to the kitchen to raid the refrigerator.

A ham sandwich and a cup of tea would suffice, and she'd almost finished both when she heard the front door close followed by the beep of the security alarm being set.

There was no way she could escape upstairs without detection, and she didn't bother to try. The slim hope she'd held that Nicos would simply ignore the array of lights on this level died as he entered the kitchen.

The mere look of him stirred her senses, and set her composure seriously awry.

A dramatic mesh of primitive sexuality and latent power that had a lethal effect on any woman's peace of mind. Especially hers.

It irked her unbearably that he knew, with just one look at her, no matter how she schooled her expression.

'A late-night snack, or did you miss dinner?' Nicos queried mildly as he crossed the room to stand a metre distant.

He took in the baggy tee shirt that reached her thighs, her bare legs and feet, and the hair she'd swept into a pony-tail. A look that was the antithesis of the corporate executive.

'You're back early.'

'You're evading the question.'

Katrina lifted the cup and took a sip of tea. 'Both,' she informed succinctly.

He loosened his tie and thrust both hands into his trouser pockets. She looked beat, and there were dark smudges beneath her eyes. At a guess she hadn't slept much in the past few nights.

Anxiety at their enforced living arrangements?

'Should we attempt polite conversation?' Katrina parried.

He looked vaguely dangerous. She tried to tell herself such a thought was the height of foolishness. But the feeling was there, in the look of him, his relaxed stance. Deceptive, she accorded warily, as all her fine body hairs rose up in protective self-defence.

Instinct warned she should tread carefully. Yet she

was prey to a devilish imp prompting her towards certain conflagration.

'How was your date—sorry, dinner?' she corrected deliberately.

One eyebrow rose with deliberate cynicism. 'Why assume my companion was female?'

'A calculated guess, given the increasing number of women in the business arena.'

'And my penchant for the company of women?' Nicos queried silkily.

'You have a certain reputation.' A statement that held a wealth of cynicism.

'I won't deny intimacy with previous partners,' he said with dangerous softness. 'The relationships were selective and meant something at the time.'

'But you don't offer fidelity. In or out of marriage.'

He didn't move, but she had the sensation he was suddenly standing much too close. 'You want me to reiterate something you refuse to believe?' he demanded silkily.

The air between them was electric. 'Why bother?' She held his gaze without fear. 'We did that to death at the time. It achieved nothing then. I don't see that it will now.'

His control was admirable, but his eyes were dark, almost chillingly still. 'If I were to offer the same query following your return from a business dinner, your answer would be?'

She didn't hesitate. 'Get stuffed.'

'An eloquent phrase.'

Katrina turned towards the sink and jettisoned the

remains of her tea. 'Forget *polite*.' She rinsed the cup and placed it in the dishwasher. 'Let's just stick with *good morning* and *goodnight*.'

'You think that will work?'

Why did she get the feeling he was at least one step ahead of her?

'The alternative is a war zone.'

'Battles won and lost?'

She gave him a long, considering look. 'It's not about whether you win or lose, but how you play the game.'

'An interesting analogy.'

'Isn't it?' She turned away from him and stepped towards the door. 'Goodnight.'

'Sleep well, *pedhaki mou*.'

His cynical drawl echoed in her mind as she ascended the stairs, and even in the relative safety of her bedroom the affectionate endearment recurred as a repetitive taunt.

Consequently sleep proved an elusive captive, until exhaustion overcame the many scenarios she plotted against him.

CHAPTER THREE

THERE was evidence Nicos had already eaten breakfast when Katrina entered the kitchen the next morning.

The aroma of freshly made coffee teased her nostrils, and she took down a cup and filled it from the cafetière, added sugar, slotted bread into the toaster, then sipped the excellent brew as she waited for the toast to pop.

A daily newspaper lay on the table, and she scanned the front-page headlines highlighting the latest criminal injustice, the fall of a major company, and touting plaudits for two councillors running in the upcoming elections.

When the toast was ready she spread it with conserve, topped her cup with coffee, then she pulled out a chair and dedicated fifteen minutes to acquiring an informative view of the day's reported journalism.

Until she reached the social pages, and found herself looking at a photograph of her and Nicos. Taken, she confirmed on closer examination, at a social function not long after their marriage. The caption read, *Together Again?*

An unidentified source confirms Nicos and Katrina Kasoulis have reunited to satisfy a condi-

tion of Kevin Macbride's (of Macbride) will. Fact or fallacy?

Anger rose, and a sibilant curse escaped from her lips.

Without pausing for thought she gathered up the pertinent page and went in search of her errant husband.

She found him in the study, seated at his desk, his attention focussed on the computer screen.

He glanced up as she entered, took one look at her expression, and pressed the save key.

'Good morning.'

Katrina threw him a fulminating glare. 'Have you *seen* this?' She cast the newspaper page down onto the keyboard, and jabbed a finger at the caption.

Someone had been busy. Given her extended dysfunctional family, it narrowed the suspects down to four. Any one of whom would take delight in presenting such facts to the press.

'You want to complain and request a retraction?'

She was so angry she could hardly speak. 'What good would that do?'

'None whatsoever.'

Suspicion clouded logic. 'Were *you* responsible?'

Katrina saw his features harden and his eyes grow cold. 'That doesn't even qualify for an answer.'

'*Who*, then?'

Nicos's silence was eloquent, and her anger took on a new dimension.

'I need to make a few phone calls. Then,' she announced between clenched teeth, 'I'm going out.'

'I have an invitation to attend dinner this evening.'

'I wouldn't dream of stopping you.'

'For both of us.'

'You can go alone!'

'An action that would cause speculation, surely?' Nicos posed reasonably. 'Given our very recent reconciliation?'

'I have no intention of partnering you on the social circuit,' Katrina vowed tersely.

'Considering my attendance is minimal, it won't be a hardship.'

'And we haven't reconciled. We're merely sharing the same house!'

'So we are,' Nicos said with dangerous softness. 'However, for the duration of one year we partner each other whenever the necessity should arise.'

'That isn't a condition of Kevin's will.'

'Consider it one of my own,' he said hardily, and watched her green eyes fire with anger.

'Don't try to manipulate me,' she warned as she moved to the door, adding as a parting shot, 'I won't stand for it.'

'Be ready by six-fifteen,' Nicos relayed silkily.

Katrina didn't deign to answer, and barely restrained the temptation to slam the door behind her.

With carefully controlled movements she went upstairs, changed into tailored trousers, added a blouse, a jacket, slid her feet into heeled pumps, then collected her bag, caught up her car keys and went down to the garage.

Ten minutes later she drew to a halt adjacent a park, withdrew her cellphone, and made the first of several phone calls.

Whilst Andrea, Kevin's second wife, coveted wealth and a luxurious lifestyle, was self-orientated to the point of selfishness, she didn't possess a vicious bone in her body. Her daughter, Paula, by Andrea's first marriage, was overindulged and a snob, but an unlikely candidate to raise her stepsister's ire.

Which left Chloe, Kevin's third wife, and her son, Enrique, by a previous marriage. Each of whom would delight in causing Katrina grief.

Katrina had contacts, and she used them ruthlessly.

An hour later she had the answer she wanted. *Enrique.* Now, why didn't that surprise her?

Her stepbrother was a smooth charmer who made it no secret that in his opinion *he,* as the only male in a clutch of associated family females, should inherit a major share in Macbride. It mattered little that Kevin had insisted each of his successive wives sign a prenuptial agreement, and had made both Andrea and Chloe aware that Katrina was his successor.

Enrique was a young man who adored the high life, fast cars and beautiful women. He had also acquired an expensive habit in his teens, one that had seen him in a private clinic on more than one occasion during the few years Chloe had been Kevin's wife.

At least she knew her enemy, Katrina determined as she put the car in gear and headed towards Double

Bay. She intended checking out her apartment, reassessing her wardrobe; then she planned some retail therapy.

There were a few girlfriends she could phone to come join her and share lunch. Except the invitation would elicit questions she had no desire to answer, and while her heart ached for the loss of her father she knew he would hate her to grieve.

Life, he had always maintained, was a celebration. And he had celebrated it well.

Yet she missed his laughter, his love. He'd been her rock, her safe harbour. In a quirk of misplaced wisdom, he'd appointed Nicos in his place.

Katrina wanted to reiterate she didn't need or want Nicos's protection. Except Kevin had played his final card and had given her no choice.

It was well after five when she garaged the Porsche and entered Nicos's home with three evening gowns draped over her arm.

She reached the stairs as Nicos emerged into the lobby, and she paused, her expression one of controlled politeness.

'Formal, Katrina,' Nicos drawled as he reached her. He named the venue, the charity, and glimpsed her momentary disconcertion as they ascended the stairs.

How could she have forgotten? It was one of the city's prestigious social events, and one Kevin had unfailingly sponsored for as long as she could remember.

She had…how long? Forty-five minutes in which to shower, attend to her hair and make-up, then dress.

She made it with scant seconds to spare, and stood silent beneath Nicos's appraisal.

The crêpe georgette gown in jade-green with its bias-cut asymmetric flounces and figure-hugging lines accented her slim curves and highlighted her cream-textured skin. To save time she'd simply swept her hair into a careless chignon, had added diamond stud earrings and a matching pendant.

As to Nicos, the sight of him made the breath catch in her throat. He held his thirty-seven years superbly, his masculine frame attesting to a regular exercise regime. Attired in a black evening suit, white shirt and black bow tie, he looked every inch the wealthy sophisticate. Yet it was his innate sexuality and an intrinsic knowledge of the opposite sex that added another dimension. One any thinking woman couldn't fail to recognise.

A year ago she would have offered a teasing comment, brushed the edge of his jaw with her fingers and placed her mouth against his in a light kiss.

Now she did none of those things. Instead she crossed the lobby in silence at his side and slid into the car parked out front.

'Should we discuss the evening's role-play?' Katrina queried as Nicos cleared the gates and traversed the leafy street.

'In light of Enrique's link to a certain gossip columnist?'

'You knew?'

He cast her a quick, telling glance. 'Did you imagine I wouldn't make it my business to find out?'

She didn't answer. Instead she examined the passing scenery with detached interest. No matter where she'd travelled in the world, Sydney was *home*.

It was a beautiful city, with a picturesque harbour and buildings of varied architecture. Possessed of a relatively mild climate, the clear blue skies and sparkling waters of Port Jackson, with cliff-top mansions and numerous small craft anchored in the many bays and inlets, provided an endearing sense of familiarity evident as Nicos traversed the inner-city streets before easing the car to a halt adjacent the hotel's main entrance for valet parking.

Guests mingled in the large lobby adjoining the grand ballroom. Uniformed waiters circled the area proffering trays of drinks, and the buzz of conversational chatter abounded.

The social élite, Katrina mused, dressed in their finest, with the women collectively displaying sufficient jewellery to fund a year's aid to a Third-World country.

There were many guests present who would have sighted the photo of Katrina and Nicos Kasoulis and its teasing caption in the morning's newspaper gossip column. Circumspect interest was expected, and she forced herself to ignore the telling glances, the quiet asides as she stood at Nicos's side and sipped a mix of champagne and orange juice.

A few acquaintances made a point of extending their condolences for the loss of her father, others conveyed silent hand signals indicating they'd catch up through the evening.

Katrina sighted both of her stepmothers standing at opposite ends of the lobby, a presence that issued a silent statement of their individual importance on the social scene. Andrea had her man-of-the-moment in tow, while Chloe was partnered by none other than her son, Enrique.

It was a blessing that Siobhan, at least, didn't try to compete on any level, much preferring a less fashionably social existence.

Three of Kevin's ex-wives at one gathering would be too much to handle. It had been bad enough keeping the peace at her father's funeral, where a farce worthy of Hollywood had been played out for the benefit of those sufficiently intrigued to observe it. Of whom there had been several, Katrina reflected grimly.

Nicos watched the fleeting expressions chase across his wife's features, and caught the determined resolve evident as she mentally braced herself for an inevitable confrontation.

Andrea and Chloe's interest in Kevin's daughter could only be termed superficial, yet each woman painstakingly observed social etiquette. Enrique, on the other hand, was something else.

'You don't have to handle it alone.'

Katrina met Nicos's dark gaze, and forced her lips into a faint smile. 'Is that meant to be reassuring?'

'Count on it.'

'My bodyguard,' she stated with an attempt at cynicism.

'That, too,' he responded with light mockery.

'Katrina, darling.'

She turned at the sound of that soft, purring voice, and went into the air-kiss routine Andrea favoured.

'Nicos.' There was a degree of wariness beneath the superficial greeting before Andrea turned back to her stepdaughter. 'Kevin would be proud you made the effort to be here so soon after his passing.'

A compliment or condemnation? Katrina chose to take the words at face value. 'Thank you, Andrea.'

Five minutes after Andrea moved away, Chloe crossed the lobby to Katrina's side.

'We weren't sure you'd attend tonight.' Sleek, polished, and very self-assured, Kevin's third wife possessed the practised aloofness of a catwalk model.

'It's what Kevin would have wanted,' Katrina responded evenly before acknowledging her stepbrother. 'Enrique.'

A young man whose pretty-boy attractiveness was deceptive, during Chloe's marriage to Kevin he'd imagined that seducing Kevin's daughter would be a shoe-in...only to discover Katrina wasn't about to play. It hadn't stopped him from trying, and he'd never quite forgiven her for spoiling his plans of a dream ride through life on the Macbride fortunes.

His eyes gleamed briefly with something akin to bitter resignation as they raked her slender form. 'You look divine, sweetheart.'

'Doesn't she?' Nicos caught her hand and lifted it

to his lips, his eyes dark and unfathomable as he silently dared her to pull her fingers free from his grasp.

Her reaction to his touch was immediate and damning, for her pulse jumped to a quickened beat as warmth coursed through her veins. It felt as if her heart was working overtime, and it took considerable effort to appear unaffected.

'What do you think you're doing?' Katrina demanded quietly the instant Chloe and Enrique moved out of earshot.

'Damage control.'

'For whose benefit?' she queried with skepticism.

'Yours,' Nicos said silkily.

'I doubt playing charades will work.'

A hovering waiter took her empty glass and offered her another, which she declined.

It was something of a relief when the ballroom doors opened minutes later and the guests were instructed to take their seats.

The food had to be delectable, given the price per ticket, but Katrina merely forked a few mouthfuls from each course, sipped a glass of excellent Chardonnay, and conversed politely with fellow guests seated at their table.

The evening's entertainment was varied, and during a break she excused herself and threaded her way towards the powder room.

A headache was niggling away above her temple, and she'd have given anything to be able to leave and go home.

Except home was no longer her apartment, and the

term of her enforced sojourn with Nicos had only just begun.

There was a queue, and she had to wait to gain space in front of the long mirror in order to freshen her lipstick.

Was it design or coincidence that seconds after emerging the first person she saw was Enrique? Considering her stepbrother inevitably had a plan, she opted for the former, acknowledged his presence, and made to bypass him *en route* to the ballroom.

One glance at his expression determined he had a mission in mind and, unless she was mistaken, he was bent on ill intent.

'I wanted to see you alone,' he began without preamble.

She could almost pre-empt what he was going to say, but she remained silent, willing to admit she might be wrong.

'I need some money.'

'I don't have any on me.'

'But you can get it.'

They'd been this route before. In the beginning, she'd thought she could help, and had. Until she'd realised she was only feeding his habit. 'No.'

'Tomorrow. Meet me for lunch. Bring it then.'

She was past feeling sorry for him. 'What part of *no* don't you understand?'

'I'm begging you, dammit!' He pulled in his temper with effort. 'A thousand, Katrina. That's all.'

'Didn't playing news gossip informant pay well enough?'

His eyes hardened. 'I don't know what you're talking about.'

Her headache intensified. 'Even if I were to lend it to you, how long will that hold off the heavies, Enrique? A week? Then what will you do?'

'All I need is one win—'

'No.'

Katrina watched his features darken with dread. Enrique in a mean mood was something she'd prefer to avoid.

His hand caught her arm in a painful grip. 'Bitch!' he exclaimed with soft venom. 'You'll pay for this!'

'Let me go,' she said quietly, and clenched her teeth against a silent cry as his fingers twisted viciously on her skin.

'Do as Katrina says.' Nicos's voice was a chilling drawl. *'Now.'*

Enrique's hand fell to his side.

'I can't think of any good reason for you to threaten my wife,' Nicos said with dangerous softness. 'Touch her again, and I can promise you won't walk or talk for some considerable time.'

'You should be aware I've instructed my lawyer to contest Kevin's will,' Enrique declared vehemently.

'Something that will prove an exercise in futility,' Nicos advised with hard inflexibility. 'Each of Kevin's wives were well provided for in their divorce settlements,' Nicos continued with deceptive mildness. 'Neither you nor Paula have any reason to make a claim against Kevin's estate.'

'That's not how I see it!' Without a further word, Enrique turned and re-entered the ballroom.

Katrina cast Nicos a fulminating look, and almost died at the latent anger evident.

'I didn't need rescuing!'

His expression remained unchanged. 'No? From where I was standing, your charming stepbrother appeared to have the advantage.'

She could have told him Enrique had used a variety of bullying tactics in the past. And that Chloe's son felt his stepsister owed him by virtue of his mother's marriage to Kevin Macbride.

Her chin lifted fractionally, and her eyes were clear. 'I can handle him.'

A muscle clenched at the edge of his jaw. 'Verbally, without doubt,' Nicos acknowledged with an edge of cynicism.

Katrina barely restrained stamping her foot in angry frustration. 'Don't play the heavy, Nicos.'

'I'll take you home.'

'The hell you will.'

'Determined to thwart me at every turn, Katrina?'

She drew a deep, calming breath. 'If we don't go back in there, Enrique will imagine he's scored a point against me.'

'Fifteen minutes,' Nicos conceded. 'Then we leave.'

It was closer to an hour, and almost midnight when they entered the house. Together they ascended the stairs, and Katrina turned as they reached the landing.

'Goodnight.'

Nicos lifted a hand and caught hold of her chin, then his mouth closed over hers in an evocative kiss that was all too brief as his tongue skimmed hers, tasted, then retreated.

For a moment it left her wanting more, and she fought against the instinctive need to move in close and kiss him back.

Except that would be tantamount to an admission of sorts, and she'd spent too many months building up a barrier against him. To allow him to begin tearing it down would be the height of foolishness. Besides, she doubted she could bear the pain.

She pulled away from him, and he let her go.

Too easily, she reflected as she reached her room and closed the door behind her.

CHAPTER FOUR

SUNDAY dawned with grey skies and the imminent threat of rain. Katrina rose early, donned a sweatshirt, shorts and trainers, went downstairs to the kitchen, made up fresh orange juice, filled a glass and drank the contents, then traversed the spiral staircase to the gym.

The house was quiet, and she entered the large room, viewed the various equipment, crossed to the punching bag and swung a solid right into its centre. Something which bruised her knuckles, but gave infinite satisfaction.

'If you aim for a repeat, I suggest you don a boxing glove,' Nicos drawled as he entered the room, and she turned towards him with a glare that merely caused him to arch an eyebrow in silent query. 'Or perhaps you'd rather hit the quarry instead of making do with a substitute?'

Had he followed her down here? Doubtful, given time spent in the gym was part of his daily routine. She cursed herself for unintentionally choosing an early morning sojourn.

'Don't tempt me.'

She looked about seventeen, devoid of make-up and her hair caught in a pony-tail. Her eyes were stormy, her mouth soft and full. He had to curb the desire to cross the room and explore her mouth with his own, aware such an action would probably earn him a swift jab in the ribs and a diatribe worthy of a seasoned navvy.

Katrina crossed to the treadmill, adjusted the settings, and set it in motion, increasing the speed to a punishing pace, then followed it with time on the exercise bike.

She deliberately concentrated her energies on achieving a predetermined number of kilometres, and was unable to stem a heightened awareness of Nicos as he spent time with various weights, the bench press, and the treadmill.

Her fitness regime didn't come close to his, something that appeared clearly obvious as she picked up a towel and began to dab the sheen of sweat beading her forehead.

Katrina spared Nicos a surreptitious glance as she curled the towel round her neck. *He* could have been taking a walk in the park for all the effort it appeared to cost him.

The flex of well-honed muscle and sinew presented a dramatic mesh of strength and power, one that was impossible to ignore. For it brought images to mind she'd tried hard to forget.

It mattered little that she'd been unsuccessful. Or that being thrust back into his presence forced her to confront an ongoing battle with her emotions.

Anger and pain warred with a primitive alchemy. One she recognised, the other she condemned.

How could she feel anything for a man who had

not only kept his mistress after marriage, but had foolishly impregnated her without caution?

Why, then, had Nicos agreed to Kevin's ridiculous suggestion? Worse, what role did Georgia play in all of this?

Dammit, there was a child involved. A baby boy who must surely be only a matter of weeks old. What of him?

There were too many conflicting thoughts chasing through her mind for easy conjecture, and with a mental shake of her shoulders she contemplated entering the sauna, then the plunge pool. Except that would mean stripping off, and there was no way she intended to disrobe in his presence.

Besides, she really needed to put some space and distance between them, and she quietly exited the room. Breakfast, followed by a shower, then she'd don casual clothes and go out for the day.

Anywhere that would take her away from this house and the indomitable man who owned it.

Twenty minutes later she descended the stairs, *en route* to the garage, and encountered Nicos in the lobby.

He took in the bag slung over her shoulder, and car keys in her hand. 'Going out?'

'You object?' Katrina countered coolly.

'Now, why should I do that?'

She made to move past him. 'Don't wait up.'

A hand closed over her forearm. 'An observance of common courtesy wouldn't go astray.'

She cast his hand a telling glance, then lifted her

gaze to meet his. 'As to where I'll be, and the time of my return? Difficult, when I have no definite plans.'

'Except to escape.'

It irked that he knew her so well. *'Yes.'*

He let her go, and minutes later she eased her car through the gates, then headed towards the northern beaches.

She could have phoned a friend and organised to share the day, but she preferred solitude and a good book.

Choosing a relatively isolated beach, she spread out a towel, switched her mobile phone to message-bank, and opened the latest paperback release written by a favourite author.

Lunch was a sandwich bought from a nearby kiosk, plus bottled spring water, and she read for a few hours, then oddly restless she packed up her belongings and drove into the city where she browsed the shops at Darling Harbour.

It was easy to lose herself in the wandering crowd, and she paused to admire a silver bracelet displayed in a silversmith's window. Its intricate design was sufficiently unusual to warrant closer examination, and she was about to enter the shop when a familiar voice greeted her. 'Slumming, darling?'

Katrina turned to face a tall, slender blonde whose attractive features had, she knew, been cosmetically enhanced. The result was perfection, complemented by exquisite make-up, and her designer apparel emphasised sculptured curves and a physically toned body.

'Paula,' she acknowledged, aware her stepsister's smile was as superficial as her apparent warmth.

'Trying for incognito, Katrina? Or am I missing something, and *this*—' she indicated the shorts, shirt knotted at the midriff, and trainers '—is a new look?'

'It's called *casual*,' Katrina responded lightly, and witnessed Paula's faint moue.

'And where is the inimitable Nicos?'

'I left him at home.' That much was true. Although how long he remained there was another thing.

'So newly reconciled.' Her smile was the antithesis of sweet. 'Although everyone knows it's only to comply with dear Kevin's last wishes.'

'Everyone?'

'Why, yes, darling.' She appeared to sharpen her claws. 'You're the lead topic among the social set.'

Doubtlessly fuelled by erroneous speculation. So what else was new? 'Really?'

'Naturally, you're aware Enrique intends to contest the will.'

'As you do?'

'Oh, no, sweetie. I have it on authority it would be a lost cause.' Paula raked Katrina's slender frame. 'How does it feel to be an heiress, darling? You always were Daddy's pride and joy. You even married the prince, only to discover he had feet of clay.' Her smile held little warmth. 'Interesting coincidence his mistress is back in town.' Her eyes widened with false dismay. 'Oh, dear, you didn't know?'

She'd had a lifetime of experience in schooling her features. 'I should thank you for the advance warning.'

'My pleasure.'

Katrina didn't attempt to qualify a reason to leave. 'Bye, Paula.'

The practised pout didn't quite cut it. 'Just when we were beginning to catch up.'

Catching up with Paula was something Katrina preferred to avoid. A personality clash, Andrea had termed their animosity from the onset.

Friendship between the daughter of one partner and the daughter of another had never been an issue. Existing in superficial harmony required wit, wisdom, and an ever vigilant eye…for the barbed comment, the embellishment of truth, and the metaphorical stab in the back. It had been Paula's mission in life to discredit Kevin's *ewe-lamb*.

Andrea's stint as Katrina's stepmother hadn't lasted long, and just when Katrina had thought it could only get better, along had come Chloe and Enrique.

And that had been worse, much worse.

Katrina spared her watch a glance, ignored the temptation to ring Siobhan, and retraced her steps to the car park. She'd visit one of the large cinema complexes, take in a movie, grab something to eat, then go home.

Except there were too many choices, and she indulged the whim to see two movies, almost back to back, with time for a snack and coffee in between each scheduled session.

It was after ten when she garaged the car and let herself quietly into the house.

Nicos emerged into the lobby from his study as she was about to ascend the stairs. Did he possess X-ray vision? Or had he added a camera to his state-of-the-art security system?

His casual attire of jeans and a polo shirt emphasised his breadth of shoulder, lean waist, and long legs.

'Did you think to check your voice-mail?'

The silky query gave little indication of his mood, and she paused, meeting his level glance with equanimity.

'Not since mid-afternoon. Why?'

'Siobhan has rung twice. Enrique, ditto, stressing the need for an urgent response. And Harry, who assured you have his number.' His expression remained enigmatic, but she detected a hint of dangerous steel just beneath the surface. 'Each of whom revealed they'd tried and failed to reach you on your cell-phone.'

'You want I should apologise for inadvertently relegating you to message-taking?'

Nicos shifted slightly, a movement that seemed to bring him too close for comfort.

She kept her gaze steady, noticing the tiny lines fanning out from the corners of his eyes, before travelling down to encompass the set of his mouth, the firm line of his lips, the edge of his jaw.

He exuded an electric stillness that reminded her of a predator about to pounce. *Go*, a tiny voice prompted. Except she was primed to fight, and viewed escape as a negative option.

'I don't owe you an explanation,' Katrina cautioned, and watched the subtle flex of sinew and muscle as he thrust one hand into his trouser pocket.

'On that we differ.'

'Go to hell.' She turned to ascend the stairs, only to have Nicos spin her round to face him.

'Don't push it,' he warned with deadly softness.

His grip on her arm was deceptive, and she knew it would tighten measurably if she attempted to wrench free of him.

Katrina looked pointedly at her arm, then shifted her gaze to meet his. 'Forcible restraint, Nicos?'

'You want all out war?'

Apprehension slithered down the length of her spine. 'Polite harmony would be preferable.'

'Then, I suggest you work towards it.' His voice sounded like silk being rased by razor-sharp steel.

'Same goes.'

He released her arm, and she moved quickly upstairs, aware that he watched her ascent. Her bedroom resembled a sanctuary, and she closed the door, then crossed to sink down onto the bed.

With deft ease she activated her cellphone, replayed the recorded messages, then she rang her mother.

Dear, sweet Harry, who was contracted to redecorate two adjoining townhouses she'd recently bought as an investment.

'Colours, darling. We need to talk. You simply cannot have blue.'

So she'd ring him from the office, they'd argue, she'd relent and agree to his choice. Their token wrangling was viewed with the fondness of long friendship.

Enrique was something else. Arrogant, persistent, desperate. A dangerous combination, she perceived as she stripped off her clothes and made for the shower.

Later she lay in the darkness, staring at the ceiling. A few days down, with three hundred and sixty-two to go. How in heaven would she last the distance?

Katrina woke late with a headache, missed breakfast in her rush to get to the office on time, and from there on it was downhill all the way through the day.

Whatever could go wrong, did. She dealt with complaints in areas that usually ran smoothly, mediated and lost to a tyrannical subcontractor who bore an elephant-sized grudge, and was terse to the point of rudeness when Enrique insisted he take five minutes of her time.

Lunch was a non-event, and at two she sent out for sandwiches which she ate at her desk. At four o'clock she took a call from Kevin's lawyer informing Enrique intended to contest the will on the grounds he was entitled to a share of the estate.

Enrique's protest was merely a nuisance factor, but it was the lawyer's duty to apprise her of the development.

The headache, for which she'd taken painkillers

mid-morning and mid-afternoon, settled into a throbbing ache that left her feeling physically depleted.

It was almost six when she garaged her car and entered the house. All she wanted to do was indulge in a leisurely spa bath, take more painkillers, pull the shutters closed in her room, slip beneath the cool percale sheets, and shut out the rest of the world for as long as it took to lose the headache and regain her composure.

She almost made it. Would have, if she hadn't had to go downstairs to search for more painkillers, as all she had left was an empty blister pack.

Nicos found her in the kitchen, looking a whiter shade of pale, her slender form wrapped in a towelling robe, and her hair tumbling down her back.

'What in hell—?'

The words were barely audible, and quickly checked as he subjected her to an encompassing appraisal.

Katrina closed her eyes against the sight of him. The last thing she needed was a verbal inquisition.

'*Hell* works for me,' she said wearily. 'Where do you keep your supply of painkillers?'

He crossed to an expanse of inbuilt cupboards, opened one, and extracted a packet, then he filled a glass with water and handed both to her.

'Headache?'

'Yes.' She freed two tablets and swallowed them down with water.

She was hardly aware that he had moved to hook out a chair until he gently pushed her into it.

'What do you think you're doing?' Bed, all she wanted was to lie down and wait for the pain to go away.

He ignored her protest as he discarded his jacket, loosened his tie, and turned back the cuffs of his shirt.

'Be quiet, and relax.'

She opened her mouth, then closed it again as his hands began working the tense muscles at her neck, then her shoulders.

Oh, dear heaven, that felt good. So good. She let her lashes drift down, and just went with the flow as his fingers worked their magic.

No one had been this kind to her in a while. Not hands-on kind. Not since Kevin had fallen ill.

Unbidden, withheld emotions rose to the surface, and the tears welled then trickled silently down each cheek.

Nicos felt a plop of warm moisture hit his fingers as he used both thumbs to massage her neck, and he swore softly, then with simple expediency he lifted her from the chair and pulled her close in against him.

If he had said one word, she'd have jerked free, but the comfort he offered was too great, and for the first time since Kevin's death she quietly sobbed her heart out.

She was hardly aware that he rested his cheek against the top of her head, or that her arms crept round his waist as she held onto him.

After a while he swept an arm beneath her knees and carried her upstairs to her room. He turned back the covers, then lay down on the bed with her, all too aware that any minute she'd realise where she was and who was with her, and push him away.

Except she didn't. The shudders shaking her slender frame gradually lessened, and she fell still. Her breathing evened out and slipped to a steady beat as she slid into sleep.

Holding her reawakened a host of memories, each of them a torture to his libido, and after a while he attempted to slowly ease himself away, only to have her murmur in protest.

So he stayed. Aware he was all kinds of a fool. For enjoying the feel of her in his arms, her scent, the soft silkiness of her hair beneath his lips.

The evening air cooled, and he toed off his shoes, pulled up the covers, and eventually slept.

Katrina surfaced through the layers of wakefulness to an awareness that, while she was definitely in bed, she wasn't alone.

Not only not alone, but her head was cushioned against a male chest, a muscular arm kept her there, and her own arm lay linked around *his* waist.

Nicos. Realisation hit, and her first instinct was to scramble out of the bed and away from him.

Then several things registered. She was in her own room, Nicos was fully dressed, and she had instant memory recall.

Maybe if she slowly removed her arm... She attempted to dislodge it, only to have Nicos tighten his hold.

He slept like a cat, aware of her slightest move,

and he'd sensed the moment she'd woken, had felt the change in her breathing, the instant tension. He could almost hear her thinking.

What he wanted was to lean forward and brush his lips to her temple, to slip a hand beneath the gaping folds of her robe and caress her breasts. Nuzzle the vulnerable hollow at the edge of her neck, then trail lower to tease one tender peak as he let the fingers of one hand brush a path to the apex of her thighs.

Early morning lovemaking, he reflected, made for a wonderful way to begin the day.

Maybe... No, he dismissed. Not here, not now. When the time was right, there would be no hesitation. But he wanted her to need him, and for that he required time. Something, thanks to the terms of Kevin's will, he had plenty of. Wasn't there an analogy that those who waited got what they deserved? He thought grimly of his aroused body, the desire, and banked it down.

Half an hour in the gym, followed by a shower and breakfast, then he'd channel his energy into the corporate day ahead.

But first he'd indulge himself a little.

'Headache gone?'

Katrina's body tensed at the sound of his husky voice, and she cautiously lifted her head. 'Yes.' All her instincts screamed a warning to put some distance between them, fast.

'You slept well.'

It didn't appear that she'd moved much through the night. Or perhaps he hadn't allowed her to. For a moment she struggled with the need to thank him for offering support. A wave of embarrassment encompassed her body at the thought of the tears she'd shed in the comfort of his arms.

She slowly rose to a sitting position, caught his amused gleam, looked hurriedly down at her gaping robe, then quickly pulled the edges together.

With an easy, fluid movement Nicos swung his legs over the side of the bed and stood to his feet. His dark hair was slightly ruffled, and he combed his fingers through it, then he bent down to collect his shoes.

'Breakfast on the terrace at eight?' he slanted, enjoying her confusion. Without waiting for her to respond he moved towards the door, and Katrina was left gazing at the empty aperture.

For a few seconds she stood in stunned silence, then she quickly turned back the bed covers, gathered up fresh underwear and headed for the *en suite*.

Half an hour later she collected her briefcase and moved quickly down the stairs. She'd just set foot in the lobby when Nicos entered it via the passageway leading from the spiral staircase connecting to the gym.

Her heart executed a double flip at the sight of him in shorts and sweatshirt, a damp towel hugging his neck, and trainers. He looked disturbingly male, all bunched muscle, and the faint sheen of sweat leaving patches of damp on a tee shirt that clung to wide shoulders, a broad chest.

Nicos took in the briefcase, the business suit, the stiletto heels, and slanted an eyebrow.

'An early start?'

'Yes,' Katrina agreed evenly. She could put in some time on the computer before her secretary arrived and the day began in earnest.

He used the edge of the towel to blot moisture beading his forehead. 'Don't wait dinner. I'll be late.'

'So will I,' she responded without thought, and stepped towards the internal door leading to the garage.

What on earth had prompted her to say that, when she hadn't planned a thing? She could ring Siobhan and suggest they eat out, she contemplated as she fired the engine and eased her car towards the gates. Maybe take in an art gallery, or a foreign movie.

The day progressed with only a few minor irritations. She contacted Harry, and arranged to meet him in her lunch-hour at the townhouses where, in typical Harry-style, he overrode her suggestions with the air of *one who knows best*.

'Muted green carpet, a mix of pale apricot, peach and shades of cream for the paintwork and soft furnishings, darling.' He caught her hand and pressed her fingers to his lips, then drew a wide arc with one arm. 'It will be truly magnifica.'

'Not blue?' she teased, and caught his pained expression. 'Okay,' she capitulated with a warm smile. 'Suppose you tell me what colour scheme you've devised for the adjoining townhouse?'

Harry waxed lyrical, as only Harry could, and she wrangled a little, because he expected it, and they achieved a compromise with which each was quietly pleased.

She had a good eye for a bargain, a knack for being able to envisage the finished product, and the two adjoining townhouses numbered her third property purchase in the past year. Each one had been completely redecorated by Harry's team of contractors, and sold for a handsome profit. As she cut him a percentage of that profit, he had more than the usual interest in each project.

'I'm looking at something in Surrey Hills.' It was an older suburb, parts of which were becoming trendy among the 'double income, no kids' set.

Harry's eyes sharpened. 'A terrace house?'

'Three, actually.'

'Solid structure?' He fired off a number of questions, then requested the address. 'I'll go check them out, and get back to you.'

He would, she knew, make them a priority, and as she drove back into the city she wondered if his vision would match her own.

Three terrace houses might be a bit ambitious, but they were in a block of six, situated in a prime position, and formed part of a deceased estate which the family wanted sold.

The afternoon was busy. She left the office late, and went directly to meet Siobhan at the small, trendy restaurant a friend had recommended. New owners, a fresh decor and an appealing menu provided an excellent meal.

The film Katrina chose was a slick Spanish comedy

with English subtitles, containing wry, often black humour, and afterwards they shared coffee.

Her mother was great company, with an infectious wit, and very much her daughter's friend, for they shared an equality that dispensed with any generation gap.

'Are you coping okay?' Siobhan queried gently as she reached forward and caught hold of Katrina's hands, the touch warm, brief.

'Now, there's an ambiguous question.' She managed a smile. 'Care to define it?'

'Living with Nicos.'

The term held connotations Katrina didn't want to think about. 'Separate rooms, separate lives.'

A succinct summary that didn't come close to describing the electric tension apparent. It was a latent force, a constant reminder of what they'd once shared, and she rode an emotional see-saw trying to deal with it.

Siobhan wisely kept her own counsel. She knew her daughter well. Enough not to pursue a sensitive subject. 'More coffee, darling?'

Katrina shook her head. 'No, thanks.' She spared her watch a glance and saw that it was close to midnight. 'I really should get—' she faltered on the verge of saying home. 'Back.'

Nicos's Mercedes was in the garage when she drove in, and lights glowed in the house.

He appeared from the direction of the study as she entered the lobby. He'd discarded his jacket and tie, had loosened the two top shirt buttons, and had rolled up his sleeve cuffs.

'Interesting evening?'

She could prevaricate and almost did, except something in those dark eyes warned against defiance. 'Dinner and a movie with Siobhan,' she elucidated. 'We lingered over coffee.' If he could question her whereabouts, she could query his. 'Yours?'

'Dinner with a client.'

'Who won?' It was a facetious query, and one that brought a faint, humorous twist to the edge of his mouth.

'I achieved a narrow winning margin.'

Of course. Nicos didn't play to lose. 'Congratulations.'

He inclined his head. 'A business colleague has issued a dinner invitation for tomorrow evening.'

'How nice for you.'

'Naturally I expect you to accompany me.'

Naturally. 'What if I choose not to?'

'I thought we'd agreed to present a united front?'

'In that case, you won't object accompanying me to the ballet next Monday evening?' Katrina countered with a sweet smile. Nicos enjoyed the arts, but that did not include classical dance.

His gaze narrowed. 'You have tickets?'

'Of course.' A visiting Russian troupe had ensured a bookings sell-out, and she'd intended to invite a friend. Now she hastily revised her plans to include Nicos.

Her smile broadened. 'It's called negotiation. A term you're very familiar with.'

'Done.'

'In that case,' she said sweetly. 'I'll say goodnight.' Without a further word she turned and ascended the stairs.

CHAPTER FIVE

KATRINA dressed with care, choosing an elegant, fitted gown in cream ecru. The intricate small crystal and pearl beading made the top a work of art, extending to the hipline, where the beads fell in measured, loose strings to the hem to swing slightly with every move she made.

Tonight she sought a sophisticated image, and she pinned her hair into a sleek French twist, took time with her make-up, and added a diamond tennis bracelet with matching pendant and ear studs. Stiletto heels lent her added height.

She had wined and dined with some of the country's social élite, and could converse knowledgeably on any number of subjects.

So why should she be nervous about sharing an evening with a few of Nicos's associates and their wives?

Because what the tabloid press hadn't revealed, gossip and innuendo would have filled in the blanks…in spades.

The interest would be circumspect, the conversation polite. But without doubt, Nicos and Katrina Kasoulis would be the focus of attention.

'Ready?'

She turned and spared him a level glance, noting

the black evening suit—Armani? Cerruti? He favoured the impeccable tailoring of both designers. His white shirt was of the finest cotton, the silk tie faultless.

However, it was the man wearing the clothes who stirred her senses. The broad facial features, dark piercing eyes, a mouth she had only to look at to remember how it felt on her own.

He possessed a dangerous sensuality that drew women like bees to a honey pot. Inherent charm and an awareness of some indefinable primitiveness beneath a sophisticated façade. Add wealth and power, and the combination was lethal.

She could understand how a woman would fight for him.

As Georgia had?

Could *she* have gone to such lengths to have his child and wreck a marriage?

Katrina mentally shook her head. A fair fight was one thing. Employing devious underhand means was something else.

'Have I suddenly acquired a few grey hairs?'

She registered Nicos's drawled query, and managed a quizzical response. 'Not to my knowledge.'

'Then, shall we leave?'

Their hosts resided in Woollahra, a gracious old home set back from the road with a magnificent view.

Cars lined the illuminated driveway, and inside guests mingled in a large formal lounge. Muted music emitted from speakers, providing a pleasant back-

ground as Katrina moved at Nic
host performed introductions.

Nicos's hand rested against the s
A proprietorial gesture, or reassuranc

Katrina accepted a flute of champag
the chilled liquid.

'I imagine we're supposed to project solidarity?'
she inclined lightly, and caught the hint of amusement
evident in the look he cast her.

'Advisable, wouldn't you say?'

'Just don't expect me to display adoring affection.'

His mouth curved into a warm smile. 'I'm disap-
pointed. Adoring affection would make a pleasant
change.'

'I'll save the animosity for when we're alone.'

'For which I'm incredibly grateful.'

'The animosity, or being alone?' It was almost fun
to indulge in harmless banter.

'Both.'

'You enjoy our heated exchanges?'

Nicos lifted a hand and pressed a finger to her
mouth. 'I enjoy watching your emotions at play.'

He was adept at discerning each and every one of
them. Right now she was nervous, but determined to
adopt a façade that only he could penetrate. It was
evident in the slightly rapid beat of her pulse, the
quick and almost too-ready smile, the depth of green
in those beautiful emerald-green eyes.

His attempt to soothe was spontaneous, a light trail
of his fingerpads across her shoulder blades, and he
watched her eyes dilate in awareness of his touch.

think we should mingle, don't you?' Katrina murmured, and took a deliberate sip of champagne. This was madness. A simple gesture, and she had to control her body's natural instinct to lean into him. 'Thea and Rafe Richardson have not long arrived. Perhaps we could join them?'

It was a pleasant evening, the food superb. The table seating arrangements proved interesting, and while the conversation flowed, accompanied by scintillating laughter, Katrina was conscious of receiving circumspect attention...from several women, whose veiled curiosity searched for the slightest crack appearing in Nicos's or her own projected persona.

If anything, Nicos seemed bent on displaying an element of *tendresse*, much to her discomfort. It was evident in the touch of his hand on hers, albeit that it was fleeting. Whenever they spoke together, and it seemed it was often, he gave the impression each word held meaningful importance. His attentiveness was exemplary.

'You're in serious danger of overkill,' Katrina relayed in an undertone as he refilled her water glass.

'Taking care of you?'

She was willing to swear he wasn't talking about *food*. It brought forth a vivid memory of just *how* he'd taken care of her needs...in the bedroom, and out of it...and her frequently explosive reaction. He possessed the touch, the skill, the knowledge, to drive her wild.

By the time dessert was served, she'd had enough. If this was a game, it was only fair she began to play.

Without pause for thought she spooned a small quantity of superb *crème caramel* and offered it to Nicos. 'Taste this, darling.'

His gaze locked with hers, dark brown with emerald green, and the firm curve of his mouth parted to accept the morsel.

She refrained from repeating the gesture, and minutes later she laid a hand on his thigh. The sudden tightening of sinew beneath her fingers was encouraging, and she dug her nails in lightly, then slowly trailed her fingertips towards his groin.

'Payback, Katrina?'

'Yes.'

'Don't overstep the mark.'

'I wasn't aware any boundaries were set.'

'Retribution has a price.'

'Threat or challenge?'

His eyes darkened. 'It's your hand to play.'

A *double entendre* if ever there was one! Perhaps a retreat was advisable. Temporarily, she conceded, for she wasn't done yet.

With deliberate intent she turned to the guest next to her and began a conversation, the content of which she retained little memory within minutes of concluding it.

'I understand you're flying down to Melbourne tomorrow to examine two sites Kevin had under review,' said Nicos.

Katrina turned towards him and contained her surprise. Her lawyer knew of her intention, and had presumably seen it as his duty to relay the information to Nicos.

'Yes.'

'I'll accompany you.'

'Why?'

'It's in my interest as joint executor of Kevin's will and a member of the directorial board to sanction any decision you make regarding the sale of estate assets,' he evinced smoothly.

'I intend staying overnight.' An intention which should interfere with his business schedule.

'No problem. I imagine you've booked the early flight?'

She wanted to gnash her teeth, and barely restrained herself from doing so. He'd very cleverly manoeuvred her into something she could hardly get out of, given that it was a legitimate business trip. But it was the *overnight* bit that irked, for the invention had worked against her.

Coffee was served in the lounge, and she sank gracefully into a single cushioned chair. Here at least she was safe.

Wrong, she acknowledged minutes later. Nicos came to stand within touching distance, and his close proximity had a measured effect on her breathing. As well as other more intimate parts of her body.

What was wrong with her? They were each enacting a part. As soon as their car cleared the gates, it would herald a return to the status quo. Separate bedrooms, separate lives. Connecting only for the sake of appearances.

So why did she feel as if her body was a finely tuned instrument awaiting the master's touch? Every nerve was taut, each pleasure pulse acutely sensitised.

If he touched her, she'd go up in flames.

Did he know? Dear heaven, she hoped not! It would be a total humiliation. Hers.

She wanted the evening to end. To be able to go home, slip out of her clothes, remove her make-up, and crawl into bed. Alone.

Liar. You want to be with him. To experience once more what you once shared together. For the good times.

With Nicos, it had been more than sex. It had been intimacy, a physical expression of love between two people in tune with each other on every level.

All her protective instincts warned any attempt to revisit that special place would be akin to committing emotional suicide. And she was a survivor. She *had* to be.

It was after eleven when Nicos indicated they should leave, and she expressed her gratitude to their hosts, bade fellow guests goodnight, and walked at Nicos's side to the car.

Minutes later they cleared the gates and soon reached the arterial road leading towards Point Piper.

Street lights provided illumination, and the tree-lined avenues cast looming shadows. Many of the houses were in darkness, but every now and again a lit window revealed activity within.

'All talked out?'

Katrina turned slightly at the sound of that musing

drawl, and could determine nothing from his expression. In the shadowed interior, his features were all angles and planes.

'In recovery mode after playing charades,' she declared, and heard his throaty chuckle.

'That bad, hmm?'

In their hosts' home there had been security in numbers. Now they were alone, and effects of the game still lingered. Yet she was conscious of an elemental danger, aware that if she didn't tread very carefully she could unleash a situation she wasn't ready to deal with...now, or at any stage in the future.

Had Nicos's affectionate attention been entirely contrived? She told herself she didn't want to know. Except there was a part of her that reacted to his touch, and it irked unbearably that she hadn't been in total control of her emotions.

It didn't take long to traverse the distance between Woollahra and Point Piper, and Katrina slid from the car in one fluid movement, entering the lobby a few steps ahead of her inimitable husband.

The click of her heels on marble tiles sounded loud in the night's silence, and her steps were quick as she entered the spacious lobby and headed for the elegant staircase.

She was aware of Nicos resetting the alarm system, closing lights, and she fought against the instinctive need to run.

From what? a tiny voice demanded. *Yourself?*

She deigned not to answer, nor even give the

thought any credence as she reached the sanctuary of her room.

Nicos hadn't attempted to stop her.

So why did she harbour the intuitive feeling he had a strategy and a hidden agenda?

To seduce her?

Why? Except to prove he could?

And he had as much hope of achieving that as a snowflake's chance in hell, she vowed as she slipped off her heeled pumps and discarded the beaded gown.

Make-up removal came next, then she donned a nightshirt and slid into bed, all too aware that sleep was never more distant.

After an hour of tossing restlessly from one position to another she pulled on a wrap and made her way downstairs to the indoor pool adjacent the gym. There, she cast aside the wrap and dived neatly into the sparkling, crystal-clear water.

Katrina stroked several lengths, then changed style, enjoying the feel of cool water against her skin as she covered length after length.

It was mindless exercise, but one she welcomed in a bid to bring on a state of semi-exhaustion that would enable sleep.

Maybe then Nicos's image wouldn't haunt her, or invade her dreams.

Her muscles were beginning to tire, and her breathing was no longer smooth or even. Time to stop, she decided as she reached the tiled edge, then rested there for several long seconds as she caught her breath and smoothed excess water from her hair.

'Had enough?'

She gasped at the sound of that familiar male drawl, and went under as she'd inadvertently released her hold on the pool's edge.

Seconds later she rose to the surface, spluttering with indignation. 'You frightened the life out of me! How did you know I was down here?'

'Sensor security,' Nicos informed. 'A modem beeps beside my bed if lights are activated inside the house after the alarm is set.'

Katrina trod water as she tilted her head to look at him. It seemed a long way up! 'So you decided to investigate.' In the reflected pool lighting he resembled a dark angel, and his navy towelling robe made her supremely conscious she wasn't wearing so much as a stitch.

There were towels stacked in a nearby cupboard, but she'd have to emerge from the pool and walk several steps to reach one.

'Are you through expending excess energy?'

'Yes.' Please, God, he wouldn't guess *why* she'd chosen a midnight exercise stint.

He hunkered down and extended a hand. 'I'll help you out.'

'One way to help would be to fetch me a towel,' she declared dryly.

'Skinny-dipping?'

Suspicion darkened her eyes. 'Just how long have you been standing there?'

'A few minutes.'

She scooped up a handful of water and aimed it at him. 'You fiend!'

Nicos rose to his feet, loosened the tie on his robe, discarded it, and dived into the pool to emerge close beside her.

'Now we're on equal ground.'

Katrina lashed out a hand, and had it caught before it could connect. 'Let me go.'

His smile held a dangerous quirk that made her instantly wary.

'Please,' she added quietly, desperate to put some distance between them. He was too close, too physical, *too much*.

'Is it me you don't trust,' Nicos mused thoughtfully. 'Or yourself?'

She swallowed the faint lump that had risen in her throat. 'I won't play mouse to your cat.'

'Is that what you think I'm doing...playing?'

Her gaze was steady. 'I think you're deriving a certain amount of amusement from the situation.'

'And you'd like to escape?'

'I'd like to get out of the pool,' Katrina corrected.

'Then, go, *pedhi mou*,' he bade. 'I won't stop you.'

She watched as he moved away from her and stroked a leisurely pace towards the end of the pool.

With quick movements she levered her body onto the tiled surround, stood to her feet and quickly pulled on her discarded robe.

She should have felt cold, for the water had been cool, but instead heat flooded her veins and her heartbeat quickened measurably as she extracted a towel and wound it into a turban over her wet hair.

This wasn't the first time she'd shared the pool, naked, with Nicos. Except then... No, she determined resolutely, don't think about *then*.

Without a backward glance she quickly negotiated the two flights of stairs to her bedroom, showered and shampooed her hair before engaging the hair-drier, then she slid into bed.

A faint groan left her lips as she caught sight of the time. In too few hours her alarm would sound and she'd need to rise, change, pack an overnight bag, and leave for the airport.

CHAPTER SIX

MELBOURNE was a vast, cosmopolitan city with wide, tree-lined streets, electric trams, and changeable weather.

It was two years since Katrina had visited, and little seemed to have changed as the cab took a familiar route from the airport.

The hotel was a modern structure on the hill overlooking the city's heart, and within minutes of checking in Katrina and Nicos rode the glass-faceted lift to a high floor.

Their suite undoubtedly had a stunning view but, whilst there was a lounge area containing two deep-seated chairs, a coffee table, a desk with phone and fax machine, there was only one bedroom, not two, of which the focal point was a king-size bed.

'If you think I'm sharing that with you, you can think again,' Katrina declared as Nicos deposited their hand luggage.

'We share a house,' Nicos reminded her, slanting a hard glance.

'But not a room,' she argued. 'Especially not a bed.'

'Afraid of me, or yourself?'

She opened her mouth, then closed it again. 'That doesn't even qualify an answer.'

He unfolded two shirts and hung them in the wardrobe, took his toiletry bag through to the *en suite*.

Katrina mirrored his actions, shaking out the slither of uncrushable silk georgette she intended wearing to dinner and transferring it onto a hanger.

She was damned if she'd share the same bed with him. One of the comfortable chairs in the adjoining lounge area would suffice. Better, she could push the two together and arrange a makeshift bed with a pillow and extra blanket.

The niggle of irritation joined a deeper, more significant disturbance in the region of her heart as the reality of sharing this suite began to manifest itself.

Oh, get a grip, she admonished silently. They were here primarily for business purposes. They'd have lunch, attend the meeting, return to the hotel to shower and change, then enjoy dinner with Nicos's cousin, Stavros Kidas, and his wife, Eleni.

Lunch was pleasant, the food excellent in the hotel's exclusive à la carte restaurant, and Katrina began to relax a little.

They didn't linger long over coffee, and took a cab out to view the two adjoining sites.

Activity on two adjacent blocks merely confirmed Nicos's independent investigation, determining without doubt the intentions a major developer had for the entire block.

'They're going to rase everything,' Katrina opined, observing two old cottages that had stood for a century. They looked vacant, and soon to follow the fate of two equally old dwellings on their eastern boundary.

Kevin had negotiated to acquire the remaining ten cottages, with plans to remodel them into trendy boutiques, thus preserving the ambience of the surrounding area. Except a large multinational corporation had outbid him, and had offered Kevin an exorbitant sum for the corner site owned by Macbride.

'I liked Kevin's vision better,' she declared. 'The low-rise glass monstrosity already approved won't blend with its surroundings.'

Nicos threw her a calculating glance. 'You've decided not to sell?'

Her chin tilted a little, a gesture he knew well.

'They've already acquired most of the block, and if we retain the corner site it will depreciate in value.' Her eyes hardened, their purpose inflexible. 'We'll sell, but at a price. They'll pay, because it suits them.' She'd done her calculations. 'I figure it's worth another two hundred and fifty thousand.'

Nicos placed a hand on her shoulder. 'Kevin would be proud of you.'

Katrina hoped so. She desperately needed to establish credence in her father's business sector. As a woman, she knew it wouldn't be easy. Nor could she afford to make mistakes.

'Okay, let's go inspect the Toorak site.'

She turned back towards the cab, conscious that Nicos's hand had slid down to capture her own in a loose hold. She knew she should wrench free, but she indulged herself a few seconds of his touch, its warmth, and briefly wondered at her sanity.

Toorak was an exclusive suburb, an eclectic mix of old money and new, established elegant homes, tree-lined avenues, and a long bustling main street filled with trendy boutiques and equally trendy cafés.

It didn't take long to confirm extensive renovations would turn two adjoining properties into leased boutiques that would blend in beautifully with their surroundings.

'Keep these, and renovate,' Katrina stated, mentally transferring the profit from one site to this one. She liked the odds, knew it would work, and could hardly wait to set the plans in motion. She turned towards Nicos. 'What do you think?'

'Perhaps Siobhan might care to have a leasing interest with a Melbourne branch?'

He was good, very good, at reading her mind.

'The legal eagle we have a four o'clock appointment with is within walking distance from here?'

It took an hour of phone calls and intense negotiations, but Katrina emerged from the lawyer's office triumphant.

'We did it,' she said with satisfaction as she preceded Nicos onto the pavement.

Her eyes sparkled, and her smile reflected her elation.

'You did,' Nicos drawled in musing correction. 'I merely sat in and watched you play.'

So he had, but his presence made it easy, a backup she genuinely appreciated. She'd learned well beneath

Kevin's guidance, but not all men viewed a woman as having equal status in the business arena, and she held little doubt that she'd have had to battle harder if she'd come to this meeting alone.

'Thank you.'

'For what?'

'Being there.'

'My pleasure.'

Nicos hailed a cruising cab, and Katrina watched it swoop to a halt at the kerb. Seconds later the driver executed a U-turn and headed into the city to their hotel.

It was after five when they entered their suite, and Katrina slipped off her shoes and loosened her jacket.

'Do you want to take the shower first, or shall I?'

'We could share,' Nicos declared with musing indolence.

'No, we couldn't,' she refuted firmly, aware of tiny prickles of alarm slithering over the surface of her skin. She had no difficulty recalling how he looked *sans* clothes: the splendid musculature of his masculine frame, the breadth of his shoulders, the taut buttocks and powerful thighs. As to the instrument of his manhood...

Don't go there, she bade silently. Her heart began hammering at the memory of how it had been between them. His skilled touch, her reaction. Dear Lord, he'd never failed to send her up in flames.

Without a further word she gathered briefs and bra, caught up a complimentary bathrobe, and entered the *en suite*. For a few paralysing seconds she hesitated, then she quietly slid home the lock.

Twenty minutes later she emerged, the bathrobe securely tied, with her make-up bag in hand.

Nicos was seated on the edge of the bed, his attention taken by a documentary on television.

'Finished?'

Katrina wasn't conscious of holding her breath until she released it in a rush several seconds later when the bathroom door closed behind him.

By the time he re-entered the bedroom she was dressed, her make-up complete, and she was in the process of securing small diamond studs to her ears.

He had no inhibition at discarding his robe, and her eyes flicked over his frame, naked except for black hipster briefs, and her stomach did a backwards flip as she caught the fluid ripple of muscle and sinew as he reached for his trousers and pulled them on. A clean shirt came next, and she dragged her gaze away as he deftly attended to fastening buttons before tucking in his shirt and sliding the zip fastening home.

The thought of previously being held in those arms throughout the night was damning. But, oh, how she longed for the comfort they'd offered. The closeness, the caring…

What was she doing, for heaven's sake? She didn't, *couldn't* want anything from the man who had betrayed her.

Yet there was some intrinsic quality existent, an inherent knowledge that defied logic.

Sexual chemistry, she dismissed as she collected her evening purse.

'Shall we leave?'

'We're meeting Stavros and Eleni in the lounge bar,' Nicos indicated as they rode the lift down.

Katrina hadn't seen them since she'd left Nicos. Had he told them about their separation and reconciliation?

'No,' Nicos said quietly as they entered the lounge. 'Although I don't doubt they've heard.'

Was she that transparent?

There was no time to cogitate Nicos's keen ability to divine her thoughts as two people rose from their seats and moved forward to greet them.

'Lovely to see you again.' Eleni inclined with a warm smile as they settled into comfortable chairs.

Nicos beckoned the drinks waiter and ordered champagne.

'This is a celebration?' Eleni queried.

'Of a kind,' Nicos agreed, sparing Katrina a musing glance.

'I was sorry to hear about your father,' Stavros indicated. 'A sad loss.'

'Thank you.'

Stavros turned towards Nicos and began discussing a mutual business deal, while Eleni leaned towards Katrina.

'I can't begin to tell you how happy it makes me to see you both together again.'

What did she say to that? 'It's been a while,' Katrina agreed tentatively.

'Georgia is nothing but a troublemaker,' Eleni vowed quietly. 'She has put Nicos through *hell*.'

Really? On the few occasions Katrina had seen him during the months of their separation he'd looked perfectly fine.

'But then, of course you would know that,' Eleni confirmed.

Katrina didn't comment, although it was difficult to contain a smile as Eleni rolled her eyes with expressive distaste.

'The woman is a *witch*.' Eleni appeared to pull herself together and change the subject. 'So, you have been engaged in business matters all day. Now, it's time to celebrate.' Eleni's features softened. 'A celebration for us too. I am pregnant.'

'I'm so pleased for you.' Katrina's enthusiasm was genuine. A child was a beautiful gift, and Eleni had wanted babies from the day of her marriage.

Minutes later they gravitated towards the restaurant. The food was excellent, the service good, and the ensuing hours passed so quickly it was difficult to believe it was almost ten when Eleni indicated they should leave.

'My wife tires easily,' Stavros explained apologetically as Nicos settled the bill.

'One minute I'm fine,' Eleni said with amusement. 'The next I can hardly keep my eyes open.'

They walked towards the exit through the hotel lobby and Stavros organised for the concierge to fetch their car.

'We will see you again soon, yes?' Eleni embraced

Nicos, then turned towards Katrina. 'Take care, Katrina.'

Their car arrived, courtesy of a porter, and within a few brief minutes they were gone.

'Would you like to have a drink in the lounge?' Nicos queried as they re-entered the lobby.

'Okay.' Anything to delay taking the lift back up to their suite.

Nicos ordered coffee, and Katrina sipped hers slowly as she indulged in the idle pleasure of people-watching. Couples, singles, young and old.

'Penny for them?'

She looked at Nicos, and was unable to gain much from his expression. 'It's been a successful day.'

'Yes, it has.'

'Can I take it as joint executor, you approve my decisions?'

'I have no doubt as to your ability to make them,' Nicos said evenly.

'Thank you,' she responded solemnly.

'I believe you've been looking at property.'

Katrina's eyes sharpened. 'I'm using my own personal funds, which gives you absolutely no reason to question me.'

One eyebrow slanted. 'I was making an observation.'

'You want addresses? So *you* can check them out?' She could feel the anger begin to rise. 'Or has your source of information already given you a full report?'

'You use Kevin's lawyer for your own affairs,' he reminded silkily.

'He contravened client confidentiality privilege?' she queried, scandalised.

'Not at all, and only in respect of commenting on your business acumen,' Nicos said smoothly.

Katrina took in a deep breath and released it slowly. 'I enjoy restoring property.'

'The terrace houses are a good investment.'

'You know about them—*how*?'

He held her gaze. 'I'm negotiating to buy the remaining three in the same block. The agent rang me this morning and mentioned my wife's expression of interest.'

Another breach of confidentiality? Or had the agent simply assumed a husband and wife were aware of each other's financial investments?

'You intend to outbid me?'

'No. I had in mind we could collaborate.'

Her interest was piqued. 'Harry would be delighted.' She hastened to explain. 'The interior decorator I use. He's very good.'

'Have him ring me.'

A waiter hovered with a cafetière of steaming hot black coffee and offered to refill their cups, which they each declined.

Katrina stifled a yawn, then rose to her feet. 'I'm going up to bed.' She was tired, and they were due to take the morning flight to Sydney.

Nicos unfolded his length and walked with her to the lift, summoned it, and within minutes they entered their suite.

CHAPTER SEVEN

'WHAT do you think you're doing?'

'Organising a makeshift bed,' Katrina informed him as she took down a blanket and snagged a spare pillow.

'The bed is large,' Nicos said with dangerous softness.

Katrina met his gaze with open defiance. 'I'm not sharing it with you.'

'Is it me you don't trust? Or yourself?'

'You,' she responded succinctly, and stepped through to the lounge.

She pulled two chairs together, facing each other, and decided it should be quite comfortable if she adopted a foetal position.

Seconds later she extracted a long cotton tee shirt from her bag and retreated to the *en suite* to change.

Hmm, not so comfortable, she admitted to herself within minutes of settling herself down. She doused the lamp, and the suite was shrouded in darkness.

Katrina reflected on the events of the day, ruminated the prospect of Siobhan's enthusiasm at opening a Melbourne branch of her Double Bay boutique…and shifted position on the chairs.

To no avail, for one hip soon became numb from

the hard upholstering. Damn. Maybe if she lay on her back with her knees bent.

How long did it take for her to decide the chairs were a no-go sleeping situation? Half an hour? She had no idea of the passage of time when she carefully manoeuvred herself free and spread one half of the blanket on the carpet.

She leaned forward to collect the pillow and knocked her elbow. A faint groan escaped her lips. Hell, that hurt.

Was Nicos asleep? She stifled the temptation to take the pillow and bat him over the head with it.

She should have insisted on two separate suites. Dammit, why hadn't she?

At that precise moment the bedroom lamp went on, and in the next instant Nicos stood towering in the archway that separated the small lounge and bedroom.

Without a word he moved forward and scooped her into his arms.

'Put me down!' Katrina vented in fury.

He did. On the side of the bed he occupied. 'Stay there,' he warned in a voice that sent shivers scudding down the length of her spine.

She bounced back onto her feet and watched as he crossed round to the opposite side of the bed. 'The hell I will!'

He threw her a dark lethal glance. 'If you want to fight, I'll oblige.' He waited a beat. 'Just be aware how it will end.'

'I'm shaking!'

'You will, if you don't get back into bed.'

She didn't move, and her eyes burned emerald-bright with rage. 'Since when did you become such a dictatorial tyrant?'

'Ten seconds, Katrina,' Nicos warned silkily.

Her eyes went to the telephone on the bedside pedestal. 'Reception can find me another suite.' She picked up the receiver, but she didn't even manage to punch one digit before Nicos cut the connection.

'Don't even think about it.'

She rounded on him in fury. 'How dare you?'

'Easily.'

Without thought she snatched up a pillow and threw it at him, only to watch as he deflected it onto the bed.

His anger was a palpable entity. The bedside lamp cast shadows in the room, and his frame seemed to loom large, his features all angles and planes.

'Three nights ago we shared a bed half this size.'

'That was different.'

He moved with the grace of a cat, his speed indolently deceptive as he skirted the bed.

Katrina took one look and scrambled across the mattress to the other side. She couldn't win, there was nowhere to go, and she fought like a wild thing as he caught hold of her, stilling her flailing arms with galling ease.

In a moment of madness she bit him, hard, connecting just above one male nipple, and registered his intake of breath an instant before she was pushed down onto the mattress.

She bucked, trying vainly to free herself, and gave

a startled cry as he straddled her hips and pinned her wrists above her head.

'Get off me!'

He held her securely, his knees trapping her thighs, yet still she arched against him, twisting her body as she attempted to wrench her arms free.

'Stop it. You'll hurt yourself.'

'Dammit, let me go!'

Her eyes were a brilliant green, dilated with a mixture of outrage and anger, her hair a mass of tumbled curls.

She made one desperate last-ditch effort, only to concede defeat. Her chest heaved, and her breath escaped in short, furious gasps. If looks could kill, he'd be dead.

He waited, watching as her breathing steadied, and his eyes were impossibly dark. There was a stillness apparent in those strong, masculine features, a leashed savagery that caused the breath to hitch in her throat.

No. It was a silent scream that didn't find voice.

The room faded from the periphery of her vision. There was only the man, the latent, magnetic intensity evident.

Primitive awareness eased the sudden knot in her stomach, and she battled the slow heat warming the blood in her veins.

A faint whimper escaped her lips, part groan, part despair. What was happening to her? It seemed as if everything had coalesced and Nicos had become her total focus.

Her body had a memory of its own, and she was

powerless to stop the treacherous awakening as passion flared.

Damn you, Nicos. The silent curse didn't find voice. *Don't.*

Except it was way too late.

Slowly he lowered his head, and his mouth brushed hers, the touch feather-light in an evocative, teasing gesture that wasn't nearly enough.

He felt the faint quiver of her body, sensed the heat, and he nibbled on her lower lip, then nipped the full centre, soothing it with the tip of his tongue before tracing the soft contours.

The strength of his arousal was a potent force nestled against the most vulnerable part of her anatomy, and sensation throbbed, primitive, urgent, libidinous.

She parted her mouth, wanting more, much more than this gentle seduction, and she moaned an entreaty as his lips savoured the line of her throat, then nuzzled the sensitive hollow at the edge of her neck.

I should stop this, *now*, before it's too late, she groaned silently.

Except she was powerless to still the deep need, the mesmeric, erotic witchery of his seduction.

When his mouth found hers again, she kissed him with possessive hunger, angling her head for closer purchase.

Her whole body was on fire, and the breath hissed between her teeth as he freed her wrists and dispensed with her long cotton tee shirt.

A swift tugging movement divested his briefs, and

she cried out as he sought her breast, teasing a tender peak before suckling shamelessly.

Her hands slid over his shoulders, caressed his spine, then she dug her fingers into his buttocks.

Now. Her breath came in ragged gasps as he sought the moistness, his touch finding the acutely sensitised nub with unerring accuracy.

She went up in flames, then cried out as he sent her higher, and she wasn't conscious of pleading with him, or begging his possession.

Nicos took her with one deep thrust, and heard her faint intake of breath as silken muscles stretched to accommodate him. He stilled, enjoying the enclosure, the tightness as she gripped and held him, then he began to move, slowly, almost withdrawing completely before surging in to the hilt.

Again and again he repeated the action, increasing the movement until she met and matched his rhythm in a tumultuous ride that left them both slick with sensual sweat.

Katrina waited for her breathing to steady, convinced she was unable to move so much as a muscle. Dear heaven. She closed her eyes, too enervated to do anything, and she groaned out loud as he gathered her close and rolled onto his back.

His hands brushed over her skin in a soothing gesture, and she felt his lips at her temple, the soft hollow beneath her ear.

It felt so good, like coming home after conquering the stormy sea.

Slowly she lifted her body, arching it gracefully as

she rose above him. She lifted a hand and tucked her hair behind one ear, then the other, then she touched the tip of her finger to his chest and traced a teasing pattern through the dark hair, pausing to tug a little before following the line arrowing down to his waist.

She felt him harden, his length expanding as she brushed a teasing path back and forth at the juncture of their connection, only to have him replace her fingers with his own.

Her pleasure was immediate, the wild surge of exquisite sensation almost more than she could bear, and this time it was she who rode him on the path to mutual ecstasy.

Yet it was Nicos who held her at the brink, then tipped her over in a mutual, spellbinding free fall.

Katrina fell asleep curled close in Nicos's arms, her head pillowed against his chest.

Throughout the night they reached for each other, satisfying needs that were alternately urgent, then slow and magically sweet.

There was a part of her that never wanted the sensual dreams of the night to end. How many times had she imagined such a night, relived it again and again, only to wake alone with an emptiness that was all too real?

But as the first light of dawn crept over the horizon she responded to the trail of fingers caressing the curve of her waist, exulted in their intimate touch, and melted into her lover's body, fitting so well it was as if they were two halves of a whole.

It was late when they rose from the bed and shared

a shower. Even later when they sat down to room-service breakfast, lingering over coffee before dressing and checking out.

The late morning flight landed in Sydney after midday, and Nicos collected his car, stowed their overnight bags in the boot, then dropped Katrina outside her office building before traversing inner-city traffic to his own.

She should have been tired, but instead she felt energised, and she rode the lift to her office, checked with her secretary, ordered in lunch, and got to work.

Nicos phoned at four to say he'd be delayed, and Katrina indicated she needed to bring work home.

'Don't wait dinner.'

'You want to ring Marie, or shall I?' Katrina queried, only to have him respond he'd already done so.

It was after six when she entered the house, and she checked the refrigerator, saw the delicious salad Marie had left for her, then ran lightly upstairs to change and fill the spa bath.

Her solo dinner could wait for half an hour while she relaxed in the pulsating water.

Not such a good idea, she reflected, as the memory of Nicos's lovemaking came vividly to mind. Even the thought of what they'd shared caused sensation to spiral through her body, and she groaned out loud as she recollected her hungry response.

Nothing had changed, she determined, then closed her eyes in frustrated resignation. Who was she kidding? *Everything* had changed.

It was almost seven when she donned jeans, a cotton top, and went downstairs to the kitchen.

The salad was delicious, and after she'd eaten it she curled up in a chair in the sitting room and used the remote to switch on the television.

She must have dozed, for she came awake at the touch of hands sliding beneath her thighs.

'Nicos?'

'Who were you expecting?' he drawled musingly.

'I can walk,' Katrina declared. 'Put me down.'

He reached the stairs and began to ascend them. 'You doubt my ability to carry you?'

She weighed little more than a child, and he wasn't even breathing heavily when he reached the landing.

'For heaven's sake, put me down!'

He let her slide down to her feet, and she moved a few paces, then turned towards her room.

'Goodnight.'

'Where do you think you're going?'

The query was quietly spoken, yet beneath the softness there was a hint of steel, and Katrina looked at him in silent askance.

'My room.'

'No.'

'What do you mean—*no*?'

'Last night—'

'Was a mistake.'

'The hell it was.'

'We...' she paused fractionally '...got carried away,' she qualified. Words, they were only words.

None of which even began to describe the extent of her emotional involvement or her reaction.

Nicos's eyes darkened. 'Is that how you describe it? *Carried away?*'

She met his gaze and held it. 'What else would you call it?'

'We share the same room, the same bed.' He stilled her protest by pressing a finger to her lips. 'It isn't an option.'

Her eyes sparked green fire. 'Since when did you get to call the shots?'

The palm of his hand slid to cup the edge of her jaw. 'From the moment we made love last night.'

She felt her insides begin to liquify. 'We had sex.'

'So we did, *pedhi mou.*'

He sounded amused, and she fought against her body's response. She didn't want to succumb to his seduction, didn't need to do battle for her own self-preservation. It had taken *months* to build up a resistance to him. Yet in one night he'd managed to tear it down as if that invisible wall had never existed.

'I'm tired.' Katrina offered the excuse in desperation. 'All I want to do is slip into bed. *My* bed. *Alone.*'

He smoothed the tip of his thumb over the soft fullness of her lower lip. 'So you shall,' he said gently, and let his hand fall to his side. 'But it won't be alone.'

With that, he turned and walked towards his room without a backward glance.

Dammit, couldn't he see she needed time to assimilate what had happened between them? That she was at war with herself, and in a constant state of flux at having succumbed to the dictates of her flesh?

In the light of day, all she could focus on was her own weakness. This man had betrayed her with another woman. Worse, that woman had borne his child.

At the time she'd dealt with it. But now, the very structure she'd carefully built was falling down around her ears.

She wanted to hate him, and told herself she did. But she hated herself more.

Katrina reached her room and closed the door behind her. There was no lock, and unless she dragged heavy furniture to bar the door, there was nothing she could do to keep him out.

She cast the double bed a pensive glance. She was darned if she'd just slip between the sheets and lie *waiting* for Nicos to join her.

There was little doubt that he *would*.

She could, however, make a silent statement. There were three other bedrooms upstairs. She'd occupy one of those in the hope it would add emphasis to her intention not to sleep with him.

Katrina chose a bedroom, selected linen and made up the bed, then slid wearily between the covers.

She should have been asleep within seconds of her head touching the pillow. Instead she lay staring into the darkness for what seemed an age, her limbs and mind as tense as a tightly stretched wire.

She told herself she didn't, couldn't, want him. Yet her body was a mass of contradictions as memory persisted in providing a vivid replay of what they'd shared the previous night.

It would be so easy to adopt a rational mindset where she simply enjoyed the intimacy of sex. *Why not?* a silent voice demanded. Just enjoy the intense pleasure of physical contact throughout the year she was forced to stay with Nicos, then walk away. Heart whole, with no regrets.

Impossible. She'd gifted him her heart, her soul, almost from the first moment they'd met. For months she'd thought she'd reclaimed them, but last night had proved beyond doubt they were his. Always would be.

She hated herself for it. Hated him.

A shaft of light pierced the darkness as the bedroom door opened, and her tense body became rigid as Nicos stood silhouetted in the aperture.

Katrina's lashes fanned down. Maybe if she lay perfectly still he'd assume she was asleep.

She should have known better. Within seconds she felt the bed covers move, followed by the faint depression of the mattress as he slid in beside her.

How long before he reached for her? Five seconds, ten?

Minutes later she was still counting, and it took concentration to keep her breathing steady.

'What do you plan?' Nicos drawled. 'A game of musical beds?'

Had he known she was awake? Or was he simply taking a calculated guess?

'Don't sulk.'

'I've never sulked in my life,' Katrina vented as she turned her head towards him, then wished she hadn't, for he lay facing her, an elbow propped on the pillow.

With a fluid movement he reached out and snapped on the bedside lamp.

The light illuminated his features, and his dark gleaming gaze held a tinge of humour...and something else she didn't care to define.

'I'm *trying* to sleep.'

'Without success.'

'You don't know that.'

He brushed the back of his hand against her cheek, then let it trail down to the edge of her mouth.

'Don't do that.'

Her eyes were dark, the hollows smudged through lack of sleep, and she was pale. He felt her lips quiver beneath his touch, and saw the pulse jump at the base of her throat.

'Tired?'

Heat began to flare in the region of her stomach, curling in an upward spiral, and she swallowed compulsively. 'Yes.'

He leaned towards her and placed his mouth against the soft curve at the edge of her own. 'Want me to do all the work?'

His hand trailed a path to her navel, paused, then travelled low to begin an intimate exploration.

'You don't play fair.' Her voice was little more than a whisper.

'Is that a *yes* or a *no*?'

He possessed a skilled knowledge that brought forth a strangled gasp as she arched against him.

Nicos swept his tongue in an erotic dance with her own, nibbled at her lower lip, and absorbed the groan that rose from her throat.

He took it slowly, seducing her with a gentle touch, so that she simply held on and allowed him to lead a path to total conflagration. *Hers.*

Afterwards he held her close, his lips against her hair as he brushed light fingers back and forth along her spine.

CHAPTER EIGHT

SPRING was the traditional timing of the springtime gala dinner, hosted by one the city's prominent fund-raising associations and headed by a media-conscious doyenne who utilised all her people skills to provide a glittering social occasion.

With so many worthy charities abounding, it was possible for the socialites to lunch and dine out with repetitive frequency, and many did. Others were more selective, choosing to grace only certain events with their presence.

Tonight's soirée numbered high on the scale of *de rigueur* attendances, Katrina acknowledged as she entered the grand ballroom of an inner city hotel at Nicos's side.

It also entailed some tactful juggling between Siobhan, Andrea and Chloe, who would each be seated at different tables with their individual coterie of friends. Somewhere in that equation would be Paula and Enrique, who retained an intense dislike for each other, but who would for the sake of social etiquette concede to present a united front...whilst doing their best to avoid each other like the plague.

Add general interest by fellow guests as to the state of Katrina and Nicos Kasoulis's reconciliation, and the evening resembled something akin to a trial by fire.

Years of practice as Kevin's daughter ensured she chose a stunning gown in pale mist-grey with a bias-cut overlay in pale blue polyester chiffon. It moulded her slender curves like a second skin, flaring out from the knee to swirl at her ankles. Tiny beaded straps were a token gesture holding the bodice in place, and her jewellery was confined to a delicate diamond necklace, ear studs, and matching bracelet. Stiletto-heeled pumps completed the outfit. She'd swept the length of her hair into an elegant twist.

Time spent perfecting her make-up ensured her *armour* was in place.

Smile, Katrina bade silently. Facial muscle strain was a small price to pay for surviving the evening.

'Preparing to do battle?' Nicos murmured as he led her towards their designated table.

'Can you doubt it?' Katrina conceded. 'There's Siobhan,' she indicated, and felt the brush of his hand at the back of her waist.

'Andrea and Chloe are seated on opposite sides of the room.'

She offered him a winsome smile. 'Then let's go do the greeting thing in order of priority.'

It was a while before they took seats at their own table, and she had the feeling as the evening progressed that they were merely players on a social stage, each performing a scripted part.

Did that encompass Nicos's solicitous attention? The touch of his hand, the slow musing smile that sent tiny lines fanning out from the corner of his eyes?

There was a part of her that wanted it to be genuine, while another part was afraid to deal with it if it was.

She had only to look at him to *see* the man beneath the sophisticated façade. The impeccable tailoring sheathed a male body in superb physical condition, which exuded an aura that was sexually primitive and intensely sensual.

Those eyes, that mouth... Oh, for heaven's sake, she chided silently. Control yourself!

The meal comprised three courses, skilfully broken up by brief speeches, and entertainment. It was while dessert was being served that Katrina took the opportunity to glance around the large room.

And felt her heart jolt at the sight of a familiar sleek dark head. The height, the stance...

It couldn't be, could it?

Even as she watched, the woman slowly turned, and Katrina sensed the blood drain from her face.

Georgia.

What was she doing here? Not so much in Sydney, but *here*, attending an invitation-only event...

Then she saw her stepbrother hand Georgia a drink, and everything fell into place.

Enrique, enraged at her repeated refusal to lend him money, had chosen to cause trouble in the most diabolical way he knew how.

Dear heaven, *why* did her life seem filled with fraught situations?

Her first instinct was to escape. Except that would play right into Enrique's hands, and she was darned if she'd give him the satisfaction.

Had Nicos sighted Georgia? Somehow she doubted it. He was deep in conversation with a colleague and, unless she was mistaken, Georgia and Enrique were beyond his peripheral vision.

Katrina sensed the moment Nicos saw her stepbrother and recognised his companion. He didn't appear to move, but she was willing to swear most of his body muscles reassembled from relaxed mode to full alert beneath the fine tailoring of his evening suit.

Almost on cue, Georgia turned slightly and, with a smile and a word to Enrique, she excused herself and began threading her way towards them.

'Now, *this* will be interesting,' Katrina declared, *sotto voce*.

'Behave,' Nicos warned, and she threw him a stunning smile.

'Why, Nicos,' she chastised sweetly, 'I intend to be politeness itself.'

There would be avid eyes watching every move, every nuance in her expressive features, she perceived.

The separation of Katrina and Nicos Kasoulis had garnered press at the time. Just as their reconciliation was gaining undue attention now.

The appearance of Nicos Kasoulis's former mistress provided a reason for titillating gossip, and it didn't take much imagination to realise the phone

lines would be running hot with comm
Georgia Burton's arrival in town.

'Nicos.' The name emerged from Georgia's
a sultry purr, while at the same time she de-
voured him. 'I was hoping to see you here tonight.'

Sure. I just bet you planned it right down to the
finest detail, Katrina thought silently as she inclined
her head in acknowledgement. 'Georgia.'

Georgia's practised pout held just the right degree
of regret. 'You haven't returned my calls.'

'I had no reason to,' Nicos informed her with an
iciness that sent shivers down Katrina's spine.

'Not even for old times' sake? We go back a long
way.'

'It's over. It has been for some time.'

Her expression was mildly calculating. 'How can
you say that when we have a child together?'

'*You* have a child,' Nicos conceded, 'whom we
both know is not mine.'

'Still in denial, Nicos?'

'Perjury is a punishable offence.'

'So is refusing to take responsibility for one's
child,' Georgia retaliated.

'Your bravado veers towards the incredible,' Nicos
stated grimly.

'*Incredible* aptly describes your sexual skills.'
Georgia shifted her gaze to Katrina. 'Surely you
agree?'

'I'm not into ego-stroking,' Katrina proffered with
pseudo sweetness.

'And you think I am?'

...na didn't bother to answer, and watched as
...rgia offered a practised smile, then turned and
melted into the milling guests.

'That went down well.'

Nicos spared her a dark glance. 'She's courting
trouble.'

'And you won't stand for it?' Katrina queried, feeling the anger stir beneath a veneer of social politeness.

'No.'

'I think I need to go visit the powder room.'

'Effecting a temporary escape?'

'Right first time.'

She'd learned from an early age to pin a smile on
her face and hold her head high... Years of practice
meant ease in acquiring a social façade. It was a
game, a pretense, and she did it well.

It helped her greet a few acquaintances as she
threaded her way through the fellow guests, to pause
and converse briefly with a one or two.

The powder room was relatively empty, and
Katrina smoothed a hand over her hair, took time to
freshen her lipstick, and was about to retreat when the
inner door swung open and Georgia entered the room.

Coincidence? Unlikely. This was a deliberate move
on the model's part to initiate a one-on-one confrontation.

She could escape, but why, when Georgia was determined to have her say?

'I imagine there's a purpose to you following
me here?'

'Of course.'

'So why don't you get it over with?'

'The terms of your late father's will must be a terrible trial to you.' Georgia inclined with practised languidness.

The game was about to commence. It took two to play, and she was determined not to lose. 'In what way?'

'Why...sharing the same house with Nicos, of course.'

Attack was better than defence. 'After he betrayed me?'

'Difficult, darling. Surely?'

'We agreed to compromise,' Katrina said steadily.

'Oh?'

'And enjoy the fringe benefits.'

'Such as?'

'Sex.' She even managed to effect a secretive smile. 'Nicos does the sex thing superbly well.'

Georgia's eyes narrowed. One to Katrina. But how long before the model evened the score?

'Agreed, darling. But can you be sure it's *you* he's thinking of at that...ah...' she paused for effect '...intense moment,' she concluded with delicate emphasis.

Too soon, Katrina acknowledged.

'How can you compete,' Georgia continued archly, pitilessly, 'when I have his son?'

'Has that been proven conclusively?'

'Why else would our individual lawyers be in the throes of hammering out a settlement and child support?'

Not so good, she conceded, aware just how the odds were stacked against her. 'And where *is* your son, Georgia? Isn't he a little young to leave with a sitter?'

'My mother flew in from Brisbane with me. Naturally I have a nanny.'

Naturally. Whatever happened to hands-on motherhood?

'If you're so important to Nicos,' she said carefully, 'why didn't he initiate divorce proceedings as soon as I left him?'

'How can you be so sure he didn't?' Georgia countered. 'A legal separation doesn't require documentation, other than a noting of the date both parties live apart. The Australian legal system recognises a decree nisi application one year after the date of separation.'

'In which case, our reconciliation has thrown a spanner in the works.'

Georgia mentally sharpened her claws and aimed for the kill. 'Not really, darling. A year isn't long in the scheme of things. I'm prepared to let him have you for a while.' Her smile was pure feline. 'After all, I'll get to keep him for a lifetime.'

'You're that confident?'

'Determined,' the model assured.

Katrina felt sickened. 'What makes you think I'll give him up so easily?'

'You did before. Why should this time be any different?' A soft laugh slipped from her carefully painted mouth. 'Oh, darling,' she chastised with pitying candour, 'you're not going to fight for him, are you? It would be such a demeaning exercise.'

'Demeaning to *whom*?'

There was a telling silence, then Georgia pursued softly, 'I play to win.'

'So do I.'

The model took a deliberate minute to check out her mirrored reflection before meeting Katrina's unwavering gaze. 'Then, we shall see who takes the prize.'

As an exit line it was a doozey.

It was several long seconds before Katrina felt calm enough to leave the relative sanctuary of the powder room and re-enter the ballroom lobby.

Nicos was standing close to one of the main doors, one of a remaining few guests, as most had already entered and were in the process of being seated.

He watched her cross the floor towards him, his eyes narrowing as he caught sight of her carefully composed features.

She was a spunky lady in many ways, but grief for Kevin was taking its toll. Georgia with her insidious innuendo was an abomination, and Enrique was again trolling for cash.

He experienced angry exasperation at the hand fate had dealt him, and impatience at being forced to wait for the resolution. Yet it was the end that justified the means.

'Georgia ensured a confrontation.'

Katrina lifted her chin and met his dark gaze with equanimity. 'Ah, you noticed.'

'There's very little I don't notice about you.'

'Well, now, there's the thing,' she commented with unaccustomed flippancy. 'I'm sure I should be flattered.'

'She upset you.' It wasn't a query, merely a statement.

'Observant, too. Please don't ask me for a word-by-word replay.'

'Katrina—'

'Let's go enter the social fray, shall we?'

'It'll keep.'

There were friends present whom they needed to connect with, acquaintances to acknowledge, and it was almost midnight before they could slip away.

Katrina sat quietly in the car as Nicos traversed city traffic and headed towards the eastern suburbs.

'Want to talk about it?'

She transferred her attention from the brightly lit street and could define little from his shadowy profile.

He'd been so chillingly cool with Georgia...for her benefit? She returned her gaze to the scene beyond the windscreen. Even *looking* at him hurt.

'Not particularly.'

As soon as they reached home she slid out from the car and moved through to the lobby ahead of him, mounting the stairs at a quickened pace, almost as if she was intent on putting as much distance between them as possible.

Which was ridiculous, she admitted silently as she reached the landing and made her way towards the bedroom.

Nicos followed, watching as she stepped out of her shoes, then she removed her jewellery before freeing the zip fastening on her gown.

'I had no idea Georgia would be there tonight.'

Her fingers stilled for a few seconds, then she slid the straps free from her shoulders and carefully slipped the gown down over her hips.

All she wore were thong briefs, and he wondered if she had any idea how provocative she appeared. Pale, satin-textured skin, slender, toned curves, and firm breasts which fitted perfectly into his palms.

He wanted to skim his hands over her hips, then slide up to cup each breast, teasing the peaks with the tips of his thumbs, then replace his hands with his mouth.

'I don't really care.' It was as well her face was hidden from him, otherwise he'd have seen through the fabrication in a heartbeat.

Then he was there, his hands turning her towards him, and he dealt with her token struggle as easily as if he were restraining a child.

There was little she could do to prevent him capturing her chin and tilting it so she had little option but to look at him.

'Yes, you do.'

His voice was a soft drawl, and she fought against swallowing compulsively, afraid the gesture would give hint to her fragile emotions.

'Don't.' The single word was a desperate plea as his head lowered down to hers, and she closed her mouth against him, only to have her lips part involuntarily at the first, slow sweep of his tongue.

It was a kiss to die for, gentle, evocative, pervasive, and she ignored the taunting little voice in her head that warned he was merely embarking on a skilled seduction.

A faint groan sighed in her throat as he reached for the pins in her hair, slipping them free with practised ease, then he threaded his fingers through its length and held fast her head, angling his own as he deepened the kiss to something that was almost an oral duplication of the sexual act itself.

Then it was too late, and she was unaware of him removing his clothes, only that he had, and she reached for him, drowning in his touch as he tumbled her down onto the bed, the magic his mouth was able to evoke, and her own unbridled response.

It was only later, much later that she rolled away from him, angry with herself for her own weakness and with him for what she perceived as his ability to take advantage of it.

'Deny what we share, if you can,' Nicos said hardily.

Her eyes assumed a fiery sparkle. 'And that's supposed to make me feel okay? You think I don't hate myself for this…addiction to—'

'Sex?'

'*You.*'

'Thank you, *agape mou*,' he acknowledged silkily, 'for the distinction.'

Katrina burst into angry speech. 'I shouldn't be

able to feel like this. It's—' words momentarily failed her '—disgusting!'

His expression hardened, and she glimpsed a muscle tense at the edge of his jaw. 'I can think of many apt descriptions,' he said with deceptive quietness. '*Disgusting* isn't one of them.'

'What would you call it, then?' she demanded.

'Sensual magic. Primitive passion. Raw desire. Meshing into something unique...for both of us.'

Dear God. In the beginning it had been all of that, and more. Much more. She closed her eyes, then opened them again. Even now, after everything that had split them apart, the emotional intensity was just as fierce. A primeval force demanding recognition.

A year ago she would have vowed it was *love*. But how could she call it that now in the face of his infidelity? It didn't make sense.

'Yet three months after our marriage...*three* months,' she emphasised, 'your obviously not-so-ex-mistress delights in revealing she's pregnant and names you the father.' Her eyes sparked green fire. 'A fact by anyone's calculation that lays the proof of infidelity squarely at your door.'

Anger moved up a notch or two. 'Hell, you must have gone straight from our nuptial bed to hers within days of returning from our honeymoon!' It didn't help to remember the idyllic, carefree few weeks they'd spent on Maui. Lazy days and long, love-filled nights.

'At the time you took Georgia's word over mine.' Nicos wanted to *shake* her. 'Did you pause to consider how that made *me* feel?' His hands fisted, and he controlled the urgent need to smash something. Soon, he would have the proof he needed. But for now all he had was words.

'Did it never at any time occur to you that Georgia deliberately set out to destroy our marriage? You, *me*?'

'Yes.' It was an honest admission, one that had been her first thought. A woman scorned could prove a dangerous threat. 'But she provided dates, places…hotels.' Receipts as confirmation. The horror of being presented with such proof came flooding back, the memory leaving her features pale, her eyes too large, too dark with remembered pain.

'I wasn't with her.'

'Dammit, she was *pregnant*,' Katrina vented. 'She had medical proof.' Her breath hitched, and she sought control. 'She showed me a copy of the ultrasound.' A video delivered to her apartment weeks later by special messenger. Vivid, cruel evidence she'd only been able to view for seconds before being physically ill.

It was too much. To think she'd behaved shamelessly and wantonly in his arms sickened her.

With a groan that was part despair, part self-loathing, she rolled to the edge of the mattress, only to have any form of escape felled before her feet could touch the carpet.

'Let me go.'

His grasp was firm, with a hint of steel should she attempt to struggle. 'No.'

She turned on him, like an angry, spitting feline.

'What do you want to prove, Nicos? Superior male strength?' Her eyes speared his, darkly luminous, and totally without fear. 'Sensual expertise?'

Something moved in his eyes, and she banked down the sudden apprehension that clenched in her stomach.

He didn't say a word. The silence stretched between them, like a taut wire on the verge of breaking. She could see the tension, *feel* it, as if it was a throbbing, palpable entity.

Then he moved, tumbling her down on top of him, anchoring her there with an arm whose hand splayed over her buttocks, while the other fisted in her hair as he dragged her head down to his.

He ravaged her mouth, conquering it in a manner that left her stunned and unable to breathe. It was a total ravishment that gave no quarter as he used the edge of his teeth, his tongue, and plundered at will.

She heard someone whimper, and was unaware the sounds came from her own throat.

It was possession. Absolute, total *possession*. Savage in its intensity, devouring, devastating. Almost barbaric.

A man teetering on the edge of controlling his emotions, bent on imprinting his image on her soul.

Something stirred deep within, an answering, compelling need that rose of its own accord, dispensing her shocked passivity and replacing it with active response.

Katrina was hardly aware of the change, only that she was meeting and matching his passion, greedily intent on giving what he'd taken, and with equal fervour.

Hard and fast, with no preliminaries. She wanted, needed the force of it, the intense, animalistic coupling with no holds barred.

She used her hands to push against his shoulders, her voice little more than a guttural plea as she arched against him, rising to cushion the moist folds of her femininity against the base of his arousal.

With a deliberate intention to tease, she rocked against him, gently at first, then slowly traversed the length of his shaft and back again, creating a tactile slide that brought a deep, husky groan.

Heat pulsated fast, heady, magnetising, as it washed in vibrating waves through her body, and she rose up, tantalising him further for several heart-stopping seconds before she took him deep inside in an achingly slow movement that tested his control as much as it did her own.

Unleashed passion flared, raw and libidinous, as they took a ride that lasted long and left them both breathless and slick with sensual sweat.

Katrina subsided against him, and sighed as his fingers traced a lazy pattern along the edge of her spine.

This…*this*, was everything and more. A special time before problems and doubt could intrude.

The lingering aftermath of erotic, riveting love-making, where every sensual pleasure-pulse had become acutely heightened in sexual intimacy.

What they'd just shared was more than just sex. More than the slaking of mutual desire.

At this precise moment Katrina was loath to put a name to it.

Nicos nuzzled a sensitive ear lobe, then took the soft flesh between his teeth and bit gently before moving to caress the curving slope of her neck, following it inch by inch to settle in the hollow at the base of her throat.

A faint moan escaped her lips as his mouth found hers, initiating a gentle exploration with a slow, evocative sweep of his tongue that stirred the lingering warmth to renewed life.

With a fluid movement he rose into a sitting position and held her loosely in his arms as he trailed a path down to her breast.

The darkened peak invited his touch, and he circled the aureole with his tongue, savouring it, before taking the peak into his mouth.

Katrina felt her body give an involuntary shudder as he began to suckle, and she cried out as he grazed the tender nipple with his teeth. Seconds later he sought the soft flesh beneath the peak, bestowing a gentle bite before moving to render a similar salutation to its twin.

She had a need of her own, and her fingers sought the dark whorls of hair on his chest, tugging a little as she trailed his midriff and followed the narrowed line of hair to his navel, caressing it before tracing a path to tangle in the soft curling triangle of hair at his groin.

His reaction was immediate as he swelled deep within her, and she touched where they joined, feather-light, tantalising, and heard his groan as he lowered her down onto the mattress.

This time he took it slowly. Building the intensity with loving care as he sought the highly sensitised nub and stroked until the pleasure mounted and her soft, throaty murmurs begged him to ease the ache deep within.

Then she did cry out as he shifted, leaving her bereft, only to settle his mouth over her navel and trail slowly down to gift her the most intimate kiss of all.

Could you die and go to heaven, and still be mortal? she thought. At what point did pain become pleasure? And vice versa?

Katrina didn't know. She was aware that it could be both. A pleasure so intense it hovered close to pain and the need for fulfilment. The sense that she could never know its equal, the acuteness so erotically evocative she wanted it go on and never stop.

Was it *she* who cried out? She, who begged, *pleaded* with the man whose skilled touch came close to destroying her?

When he entered her, it was almost a relief, and she welcomed him, willing the intensity to lessen, only to have it rebuild and escalate as he took her to the heights, and beyond.

This time she wasn't alone, and she heard his exultant groan as he reached his own climax, and she savoured the moment, loving his passion and the joy of sharing it.

Afterwards she might analyse and dissect, but for now she was content to live for the moment.

And that was Nicos. Held in his arms, her cheek buried against the curve of his shoulder, she heard the strong, steady beat of his heart, felt the strength of his large muscled body, and savoured the comforting warmth of his breath as it stirred her hair. A stray hand skimmed lightly over her waist and settled possessively on her hip.

She loved his scent, the faint muskiness of his skin. The flex of muscle and sinew beneath the satin smoothness of its olive texture. The subtle tang of his exclusive cologne that always seemed to linger, the result of layering the same expensive brand with matching soap and deodorant.

There was something in the way he cupped his hand…beneath her elbow, her chin, curving over her shoulder. A light possessive touch that claimed her as his own.

And the simmering passion evident in his dark eyes. The look that made mere words fade into inadequate comprehension.

Once, in the beginning, she had only to meet his gaze to *know*. To nurture that need, to be aware when they were alone the night really began…a long night of loving, pleasuring each other until sleep claimed them and they woke to a new day's dawn.

Could it ever be that way again?

Complete and utter trust. Total fidelity. Because together, they were twin halves of a whole. Two hearts beating together. One soul, one love.

At the time, she'd thought nothing could come between them. *No one* could ever tear what they had asunder.

Yet someone had, and the spectre that was Georgia remained.

CHAPTER NINE

'RISE and shine.'

Katrina heard the words, lifted her head and groaned, then rolled onto her stomach and buried her head beneath the pillow.

'It's the middle of the night,' she protested in a muffled voice.

'Nine o'clock,' Nicos informed her with amusement. 'You get to have breakfast in bed, then we're driving into the Blue Mountains for a picnic.'

She wasn't sure which surprised her the most...breakfast in bed, or— 'A picnic?' she queried as she removed the pillow and turned to look at him. 'Are you mad?' It might be spring, but it was still cool. And several degrees cooler in the mountains comprising the Great Dividing Range.

The mattress depressed as he sank into it, and the aroma of freshly brewed coffee, toast, and...was that bacon?

Orange juice, too. She levered her body into a sitting position and bunched a pillow behind her back.

'This is decadent,' Katrina began as she plucked a glass of juice from the tray and took half the contents in one long swallow. She cast him a suspicious glance. 'What do you want?'

He swung long legs onto the bed, copied her action

with the pillow, then began to do justice to a plate of eggs, bacon and toast. 'I couldn't prepare breakfast and serve it in bed out of the goodness of my heart?'

He had already showered and dressed, and she silently cursed him for appearing so refreshed and vital at this hour of the morning, while she felt like something the cat had dragged in. Hair a riotous tumble, naked, and needing, she admitted silently, at least another hour's sleep.

'No,' Katrina declared with stunning succinctness.

'You malign me. I remember a few occasions when I brought you breakfast in bed.'

'Yes,' she agreed. 'Except you were contriving to keep me in bed, not persuade me to get out of it.'

'I thought we could get away for the day, take in the scenery, pick up some lunch, and have a break.'

She finished the juice, and forked some bacon into her mouth. Was it possible to maintain light-hearted camaraderie? To cast aside lingering animosity and—uppermost—attempt to dismiss Georgia for a day?

'No phones, no interruptions, no pressures,' he continued.

'We each have a cellphone,' she reminded him cynically.

'So, we have any calls go to message-bank.'

'It'll be cold in the mountains.'

'I could be persuaded to change my mind if you prefer to stay in bed.'

'A picnic sounds great,' she capitulated with alacrity, and heard his amused chuckle.

What was the alternative? A repeat of last Sunday?

Or did she contact a friend and organise time spent exploring The Rocks with its many craft shops and food stalls? Maybe arrange time on the court at a private tennis club? Or did she bury herself in work on the laptop?

There were many choices, none of which held much appeal.

Besides, an entire day spent in Nicos's company could help put their enforced relationship in perspective.

What perspective? Katrina mentally derided as she showered, then dressed in jeans and a rib-knit top.

It was nine days since she'd moved back into his home, and already she was sharing the same room, the same bed. Despite her voiced avowal to the contrary.

So what did that say about her? That she was weak-willed and malleable? Or merely enjoying the fringe benefits of their relationship?

Neither was true, she dismissed, as she pulled on socks and slid her feet into trainers.

There was a part of her that wanted to block out the turmoil Georgia's reappearance had caused. The woman's timing was masterful. Contrived to destroy any chance of what she perceived could lead to a genuine reconciliation?

Was that Georgia's aim?

Dear heaven. Was the woman desperate enough to resort to deliberate subterfuge?

Katrina didn't like the way various scenarios were swirling through her brain, and she resolutely put them on hold as she slung a sweater over her shoulders and knotted the sleeves together in front.

She intended to seize the day, and enjoy it as best she could…without introspection or censure.

Nicos took the Great Western Highway to Katoomba, passing through various small towns which often seemed to merge. There they picked up filled rolls, fruit, bottled water, and drove on through precipitous valleys, taking a turn-off leading to a picturesque waterfall where they stopped to have lunch.

Nicos took a rug from the car and spread it on the grassy verge. They sank down comfortably, and began eating in companionable silence.

It was cool, much cooler than Sydney, the peace and tranquillity a direct contrast to city living. It was possible to almost *hear* the silence beyond the soft rush of water spilling down the rock face.

The isolation was complete, and it wasn't difficult to imagine another time when life was reduced to carving out an existence, rising with the dawn to take from the day as much as humanly possible.

The evolution of man had advanced into the twenty-first century, but the beauty of nature abounded, often stark, frequently simple…a pertinent reminder of a primitive power.

Katrina finished her ham and salad roll, and bit into an apple.

'Thanks,' she said quietly.

'For bringing you here?'

'Yes.' She could feel the tension of the past few weeks begin to ease, and a sense of peace invade her being. The city seemed far distant, as did the stress of everyday living, Enrique's demands...*Georgia*. Even her aggression with Nicos temporarily ceased to exist.

He capped his bottled water, and stretched out. His jeans were a soft denim that moulded his legs and clung lovingly to his hips. A thick sweater covered his polo shirt, accentuating his breadth of shoulder, the depth of his chest.

Katrina finished her apple, then rose to her feet, only to have Nicos capture her hand.

'There's no rush.' He tugged her down beside him. 'Rest for a while.'

She *was* tired, and perhaps if she closed her eyes for half an hour...

'Time to leave. It's going to rain very soon.'

She opened her eyes, saw the overcast sky, registered the rug draped over her incumbent form, and stood to her feet. 'What time is it?'

Much later than she thought. She'd slept for more than an hour.

A light, misty rain could be seen shrouding the ranges, and soon after Nicos set the car in motion rain began splattering the windscreen. The green foliage took on a dark blueish-green tinge, and once they'd traversed the mountain and reached the valley below the mist cleared and there was sunshine.

For some reason Katrina felt reluctant to have the day end and return home.

'How do you feel about strolling round The Rocks and eating pizza alfresco?' he asked.

She turned towards him as they entered the city fringes. 'Done,' she agreed with an impish smile.

It became a pleasurable few hours as they examined the many craft and novelty shops, the restaurants and outdoor cafés abounding at the popular Rocks area, topped by the best pizza she'd ever tasted washed down with a glass of wine and followed by strong, sweet black coffee.

There was a sense of anticipation, an expectancy of how the evening would end as Nicos garaged the car, and Katrina entered the house at his side, then ascended the stairs to their room.

By tacit agreement they showered together, taking their time then, both towelled dry, Nicos led her to the bed, tumbling her down onto it with him. A husky chuckle emerged from his throat as she rolled on top of him.

Tonight was his, to pleasure and gift him the ultimate in sensual arousal. His skin tasted of soap and male muskiness as she trailed her lips from the edge of his mouth down the column of his neck, laving each nipple before travelling low...to tantalise the most vulnerable part of his anatomy with her lips, tracing his shaft with the tip of her tongue, and rendering a trail of soft kisses from groin to its acutely sensitive tip.

Nicos's groan urged her on to take an even greater liberty, and she embarked on a sensual tasting that drove him almost to the edge of control.

Then it was she who cried out as he returned the favour, lingering until she went wild and begged his possession.

Long afterwards they lay together, limbs tangled, her head pillowed against the curve of his shoulder as he buried his lips in her hair.

It was late morning before Katrina checked her voice-mail for messages: Siobhan, suggesting lunch one day through the week; Enrique, demanding she return his call urgently, followed by a second call with a similar request; Harry, who waxed eloquently about soft furnishings and request he discuss them with her over lunch the next day; and messages from two friends suggesting lunch.

She returned each of them, then got on with the day. Allocating, delegating, deferring, with an efficiency that had earned Kevin's respect. Estimates had been faxed through regarding her plans for the Melbourne site, and she tended to those, checking details and figures with close scrutiny.

For once she managed to leave the office at five, although there appeared little advantage as she sat stationary in stalled traffic, a delay which meant she didn't reach Point Piper until almost six.

Consequently there wasn't time for the leisurely shower she'd planned, and choosing something to wear to dinner and the ballet didn't permit much deliberation.

A bias-cut gown in three layered lengths of red, cyclamen and pink...colours which should have been at variance with her auburn hair, but contrarily complimented it.

Make-up complete, she caught up an evening purse and emerged to find Nicos waiting for her, looking his attractive best in a dark evening suit, white shirt and black bow tie.

The mere sight of him sent a jolt of sensual electricity through her body, and his slow smile made her ache for his touch.

Dinner was a hurried meal eaten at a Double Bay restaurant, and they waived a starter, settled on a main course, and declined dessert in order to reach the theatre before the first act began.

Swan Lake was a graceful, classical style, the music hauntingly beautiful as the dancers completed their practised moves to a level of breathtaking perfection.

One act followed another, each performed with superb artistry, and Katrina experienced a sense of disappointment when the curtain came down at the close of the final act.

Clearing the theatre and reaching their car took a while, and afterwards Nicos drove to Double Bay where they lingered over lattes and watched the social set at play.

Katrina mused that she and Nicos had sat at this particular sidewalk café during their brief courtship, and after their marriage.

It had been a favoured way to end an evening out. Almost as if they were deliberately lengthening the anticipation of what was to come. All it used to take was a look, Nicos would settle the bill, and together they'd stroll hand-in-hand to the car. Lovemaking had been a delight, for their shared intimacy had been borne out of *love*, rarely lust...although she'd exulted in the occasions Nicos had barely held onto control.

'Pleasant thoughts?'

Nicos's voice intruded, and she cast him a solemn glance. 'Varied,' she responded succinctly, and watched the edges of his mouth curve into a warm smile.

'Shall we leave?'

It was close to midnight when they arrived home, and Katrina made little protest as Nicos undressed her, then took her into his arms.

Their lovemaking was slow, almost gentle, and afterwards she curled in against him and slept until morning.

Nicos had already left when Katrina woke, and she showered, dressed, then ate a light breakfast before driving into the city office of Macbride.

She booted up the computer and got to work, frowning with vexation as the phone provided a constant interruption to the data she was intent on checking.

Consequently when it rang again she automatically reached for the receiver and intoned her usual businesslike greeting.

'We should do lunch.'

Katrina heard the words, recognised her stepbrother's voice, and cut straight to the chase. 'There would be no point in it,' she refuted evenly. 'Besides,

I have an appointment to lunch with a colleague.' A slight stretch of the truth, and one Harry would adore.

'I have some interesting information regarding Nicos,' Enrique revealed.

'Which you'll divulge for a price?'

'You know me well.'

Too well. 'If I wanted an account of Nicos's movements, I'd hire a private detective.'

'Why hire a professional when you have me, darling,' he responded smoothly.

'Goodbye, Enrique,' she concluded with resignation.

'Nicos is in Brisbane with Georgia.'

Did a heart stop beating, then race into overdrive? She was willing to swear hers did. Nicos had said nothing at breakfast about flying interstate. Nor had he intimated he'd be late home for dinner.

'Ring his office, if you don't believe me.'

'I don't have time for this.'

'But you're curious.'

Curious was too tame for what she was feeling right now. *Angry* came close.

'You have my cellphone number,' Enrique taunted.

She ended the call, and endeavoured to focus her attention on a compilation of figures on the computer screen.

It didn't work. Her concentration was shot, and after making a third mistake she pressed the save key and dialled Nicos's private line, only to hear a recorded message refer the caller to his cellphone.

Which could, Katrina rationalised, simply mean

that he was in an important meeting or out of the office.

With an effort she returned her attention to the work at hand, only to redial the number half an hour later and receive the same response.

Dammit, this was ridiculous. *Phone him*, then get on with the day!

Nicos answered on the second ring, and his caller ID negated the need for verbal identification.

'Katrina. Something wrong?'

Considering she never rang him, it was a reasonable assumption.

'Enrique is negotiating information,' she said without preamble.

'And you opted to go straight to the source.'

His voice was a cynical drawl that sent a shivery sensation slithering the length of her spine.

'Yes.'

'I took the late morning flight to Brisbane with my lawyer to personally expedite certain legal matters.'

Her stomach tightened painfully. 'With Georgia.' She didn't even voice it as a query.

'Yes.'

Had she expected him to lie to her? 'Thank you for the clarification,' she said with icy politeness, and cut the connection.

Seconds later the phone rang, and she refused to answer.

With cold-hearted determination she finished the day's work, cleared her desk, caught up her laptop, and left the office ahead of her usual time, amazed that she felt so calm.

Katrina took her car up to street level, then headed towards Double Bay and checked into the Ritz-Carlton hotel.

One night alone wouldn't contravene the terms of Kevin's will, she concluded as she glanced around the luxuriously fitted suite. There was everything at her fingertips. She could work from her laptop, order in a meal, and screen any incoming calls on her cellphone.

There was a certain pleasure in calculating the time it would take Nicos to arrive home and discover her absence. How long before he made the first call? Seven o'clock?

Fifteen minutes past, Katrina saw with a degree of satisfaction. She'd changed out of her clothes, phoned her mother, taken a shower, donned the hotel's courtesy bathrobe, and had eaten a light meal delivered by room service.

She ignored the insistent peal before the call switched to message-bank. His voice when she played it back was curt and controlled.

Half an hour later he called again, and this time there was a degree of anger evident.

By now he would have rung her apartment, and probably Siobhan, who on strict instructions from her daughter, would deny any knowledge of Katrina's whereabouts.

At what point would he give up?

Not easily, she determined, as she checked the digital screen on her cellphone before taking a call from her mother.

'Darling,' Siobhan chided gently. 'This is most unwise of you.'

'A temporary lack in wisdom isn't that big a deal,' Katrina assured her, and heard her mother's sigh.

'Nicos doesn't know where you are, and you're not answering your phone.' There was a brief pause. 'At least let him know you're safe.'

Siobhan had a point. 'If he rings again,' she agreed in capitulation.

'He isn't a man with whom any sensible woman plays games,' her mother warned.

'I'm not feeling particularly *sensible* right now.'

'Take care, Katrina.'

As an exit line it held connotations she didn't want to examine, and for the first time in several hours she felt the first prickle of unease.

Something that seemed to magnify when her cellphone pealed fifteen minutes later.

Nicos.

She activated the call, and forced her voice to remain cool, steady, as she relayed, 'I'm fine. I'll be home tomorrow night.' And cut the connection.

When it rang again, she didn't answer.

She attempted work on her laptop, then gave it up after a frustrating half hour, opting instead to check the television programs.

Choosing an in-house movie, she adjusted the pillows and slid into bed.

The stark realism of the action theme suited her

mood, and superb acting added another dimension, capturing her attention almost to the exclusion of all else.

The sudden double knock on the door startled her, and she banked down a momentary stab of fear.

Then common sense overrode apprehension. This was a first-class hotel with tight security.

The assurance didn't do much for her composure, and she crossed to the door, checked the safety latch was in place, and demanded identification.

'Room service, ma'am.'

Katrina opened the door a crack to see a uniformed waiter bearing a tray. 'I didn't order anything.'

'As you didn't use the dining room this evening, ma'am, complimentary evening tea is provided.'

She welcomed the service. 'Just a moment.' It only took seconds to release the latch, then pull open the door.

Big mistake. Nicos materialised behind the waiter, looming like a dark angel bent on castigation.

It was too late to slam the door. One glance at Nicos's expression was enough to realise he wouldn't allow something as simple as a locked door stand in his way. He'd bribed the hotel staff to organise a waiter to deliver tea. To have a porter, or even the hotel manager, request entry for one valid reason or another wouldn't present much of a problem.

The waiter, undoubtedly *au fait* with almost *any* situation, didn't so much as blink as he entered the suite and placed the tray on a table before retreating with decorous speed.

Katrina waited until the door closed behind him before turning towards Nicos.

'What in *hell* do you think you're doing here?'

Her face was scrubbed free of make-up, her hair a mass of curls tumbling to her shoulders, and her eyes were sparking green fury.

The complimentary towelling robe was too big, too long, and looked incongruous on her slender, petite frame.

Given another occasion, he might have been amused. Now, he was treading a fine line between anger and rage.

He advanced into the room, and stood regarding her with ruthless appraisal. 'I might ask you the same question.'

His voice was quiet, controlled, and much too dangerous for her peace of mind.

'I wanted a night alone,' Katrina qualified.

'Let's take this home, shall we?'

'I'm not going anywhere.'

Nicos didn't move, but she felt his presence had suddenly become an ominous threat.

'We can do this in a civilised manner. Or I can carry you kicking and screaming down to the car.'

Her hands closed into fists. 'You wouldn't dare.'

'Try me.'

'I'll call hotel security.'

He indicated the phone resting on the bedside pedestal. 'Go ahead.'

'Nicos—'

'Five minutes, Katrina. Change into your clothes or remain as you are. The choice is yours.'

'No.'

'It's not open to negotiation.'

She swore, and saw one eyebrow lift as speculative amusement temporarily overrode anger.

'Four and a half minutes...and counting,' he relayed coolly.

He could count as much as he wanted, but she had no intention of moving an inch.

They faced each other, like two opposing warriors bent on conquest. Who would win was a foregone conclusion. He had the height and the strength to overcome her with minimum effort.

Which he did, when the time was up. Gathering up her laptop and bag, he collected her business suit, shoes, and flimsy underwear in one hand, then he hauled her over one shoulder as if she weighed little more than a child.

It didn't prevent her from balling her fists against his back, nor attempting to kick any part of his anatomy where she could connect.

'You *fiend*! Put me down!'

He turned towards the door, and she hit him again for good measure. 'If you *dare* to walk out of here like this, I'll kill you,' Katrina vented furiously.

'You had your chance to leave with dignity.'

Dear heaven. *'Nicos—'*

Except it was too late.

Please God, don't let anyone be in the corridor, or the lift.

The corridor was empty, but the lift was not.

'Oh, my,' a feminine voice said quietly, while the man at her side spared a faint chuckle.

'He's a wolf in sheep's clothing,' Katrina accused vehemently, landing a hard fist against Nicos's ribs for good measure.

Was there no end to her humiliation?

'Some wolf. Some fantasy.'

Did she detect *envy* in the woman's tone?

The lift slid to a gentle halt, and Katrina was carried unceremoniously to where Nicos had parked the Mercedes.

'I have my own car.'

'You imagine I'll let you drive it?' He released the alarm and opened the passenger door. 'I'll arrange to have it picked up in the morning.'

'I'll need it to go to work.'

He tossed her clothes onto the back seat along with her bag, then placed the laptop on the floor before sliding her down onto the cushioned leather.

'So, I'll drive you.' He released the seat belt and leaned over her to clip it in place. Then he closed the door and crossed round to slip in behind the wheel.

'You're the most arrogant, *impossible* man I've ever met!'

He fired the engine, then speared her a dark glance. 'Save the name-calling until we get home and I can deal with it.'

Katrina retreated into silence, and didn't offer a word when Nicos drew the car to a halt in the garage.

With considerable dignity she exited the front seat,

collected her gear, and strode into the house ahead of him.

Savoir-faire was difficult, given the towelling bathrobe's hem trailed the floor, the folded-back sleeves had long become unfolded and hung down past her fingertips, and the cross-over front edges were in danger of parting. As to the waist tie…forget it!

She discarded the laptop on one of the wall tables in the lobby, aware Nicos was right behind her.

'Let's take it in the lounge, shall we?'

Katrina halted mid-step, and turned to face him. 'What's wrong with right here?' She dropped her bag, placed her clothes down beside it, then tugged the edges of the robe into place, and fastened the tie belt.

She resembled a belligerent child playing dressing up, he mused, fighting a need to verbally flay her for giving him a few of the worst hours in his life.

'Suppose you explain why you hung up on me, refused to take my calls, didn't bother leaving a message, weren't home, and left me to conduct a wild-goose chase in order to track you down?'

A hand lifted and she began counting off each query in turn with an angry indignance that grew by the second.

'It should be self-explanatory! You declined to tell me you were flying to Brisbane, presumably with the express purpose of seeing Georgia *and* your son.' Her eyes glittered with fury. 'I had to be informed of it by Enrique…a fact you confirmed. How do you think I felt?'

'So you decided to run away.'

'I did not *run away*!'

'What else would you call booking into a hotel and leaving me no word of where you were?'

'Dammit, I was so angry, I wanted to *hit* you!' she cried, wanting to rail her fists against him. For hurting her afresh.

'If you'd taken one of my calls—'

'You could have explained?'

'Yes.'

Her chin tilted. 'Told me what you thought I wanted to hear?'

'The truth.'

'Which is?'

'Months of legal dialogue are about to reach a conclusion.' His eyes darkened measurably. 'Georgia won a reprieve during her pregnancy against DNA testing to prove paternity. With the birth, that reprieve has been negated.' Frustration became evident, and he banked it down. 'There was a delay in the results being given to my legal representative. Today's meeting between both lawyers was an effort to expedite the release of that information.' He waited a beat. 'I went along in the hope of adding some weight to legal argument.'

'And were you successful?'

'It may take a few more days.'

'At the time you asked me to believe Georgia was a psychotic whose jealousy got so out of hand she became pregnant by someone else and named you as the father in a deliberate attempt to break up our marriage,' Katrina relayed, vividly recalling the photos, dates, that Georgia had presented as proof of her affair with Nicos. 'I didn't buy that story at the time...' she took a deep breath and let it out slowly '...any more than I buy it now.'

'Your trust in me is heart-warming.'

All the anger and pain rose to the surface. 'Damn you, Nicos. She was your mistress for more than a year!'

'A relationship that was over long before I met you.' He paused, his gaze lancing hers. 'If, as she claims, she was the love of my life...why did I marry *you*?'

'My prospective inheritance?'

His eyes darkened with glittering rage, and for one brief second she thought he might strike her. A muscle tensed at the edge of his jaw as he sought control.

'Get out of my sight before I do something regrettable,' Nicos demanded in a tight bitter voice that caused her stomach to knot with apprehension.

For a heart-stopping second she hesitated, and he ground out, 'Go. Or, by the living God, you'll wish you'd never been born.'

Katrina remained where she was. It was a matter of strength. *Hers*. Mentally, emotionally. And she refused to slink away from him in fear.

'*Fool*,' he said with chilling softness.

In one swift movement he lifted her over one shoulder and strode upstairs. Restrained violence emanated from his taut frame, and his hands were hard on her soft flesh as he released her unceremoniously down onto the large bed they shared.

He discarded his jacket, tore off his tie, and she watched in mesmerised fascination as his shoes and trousers followed. Then his shirt, and lastly his briefs.

A naked, gloriously aroused male, slim-hipped, superb musculature, he resembled a powerful force as he followed her down onto the bed.

His hands reached for her robe and dragged the edges apart, then he lowered his head and feasted on her breasts in a manner that caused her to whimper as he crossed the line between pleasure and pain.

There were no preliminaries as he took her in one powerful thrust, and she cried out as he plunged deep, then withdrew to plunge even deeper. Repeating the action again and again.

This…this was an annihilation, a primitive, no-holds-barred mating that spared no thought to seduction or pleasure. Only the need to slake a raw, barbarous hunger.

He roused in her a matching anger, and she reared up and sank her teeth into the muscle surrounding one male nipple…and heard his husky growl: his revenge was merciless, and she was repaying it in kind.

It was her only victory as he straddled her and pushed her arms above her head. Helpless, powerless, she tossed her head from side to side as he held her captive and branded her his own.

With each grazing bite, her muscles tightened around him, the spasms increasing in intensity until they merged as one.

It was more than she could bear, and she began to plead, then beg, willing him to stop. He did, emptying himself into her in a shuddering climax, then in one fluid movement he rolled onto his back, taking her with him.

She wanted to disengage and scramble to the outer edge of the bed, except he pulled her down against him and held her close.

His breathing was equally rapid as her own, and she lay still, her eyes closed against the sight of him, her mind blanking out the ravaged, almost savage, sex.

Nicos held her throughout the night, and when she thought he slept she slowly shifted her body, only to have him anchor her in close against him.

CHAPTER TEN

KATRINA woke to find she was alone, and for a moment she lay still as images of the previous night emerged, haunting her with their pagan intensity.

Nicos's hunger had been wild, unprincipled...without consequence or thought except to assuage a primeval need.

His controlled anger was infinitely more formidable than if he'd raised his voice or had resorted to smashing an inanimate object. Of which there were a few exquisite antique pieces positioned on beautiful rosewood chests flanking the lobby.

She shifted position, tentatively stretching her body...and felt the slight pull of ill-used muscles. There was an ache deep within, a remnant of his possession, and she was conscious of the sensation with each move she made.

What time was it? She rolled onto her side to check the digital clock, then sat upright in shocked surprise. *Eight?*

That left her thirty minutes in which to shower, dress, and fight traffic in order to arrive at the office on time.

She made it downstairs, caught up her laptop, her bag, and turned towards the front door...only to come to a faltering stop as Nicos emerged into the lobby.

For a moment she stood completely still, her gaze trapped in his as he closed the distance between them.

When he almost reached her, her defence mechanism kicked into place and she found her voice.

'I'm already late.'

'In which case, a few more minutes won't make any difference,' he ventured silkily.

She wanted out of here, with space between them and time caught up with the mundane routine of business to occupy her mind. 'I have to leave.'

'No,' Nicos countered quietly. 'You don't.' He lifted a hand and caught hold of her chin, tilting it to examine her features.

He doubted she'd slept any better than he had. How many times had he soothed her restless form through the night, while battling his own demons?

It mattered little that she'd provided provocation. His reaction to it was inexcusable.

'What do you want?'

Now there was a question to which he could find no single answer. Uppermost was the most important one by far. He stroked the tip of his thumb over the full curve of her lower lip. 'Are you all right?'

'Do you care?' The retaliatory words were out before she could stop them.

'Yes.'

She was powerless to prevent the faint quivering sensation that shook her slim frame. 'I don't have time for a post-mortem.'

Nicos dropped his hand. 'Tonight.'

Katrina stepped back a pace, then skirted his tall

frame. 'Before, during, or after we've attended the art exhibition?' She saw his eyes darken, and was unable to resist querying sweetly, 'You can't have forgotten?'

'No. I've already checked the day's diary.'

She turned as she reached the passageway leading through to the garage. 'I could be late.'

It became the day from hell. Traffic was backed up due to an accident, trebling the usual time it took to reach the city. Consequently it was after nine when she walked into her office.

To discover the computer network was down, and several irate messages from a client company whose head honcho wanted Macbride to supply top quality work for a cleverly worded contract worth peanuts.

There were, Katrina fumed, still men who imagined they could slip anything by a colleague simply because of her gender. She made the call, confounded him with figures and logic, then icily informed him Macbride was not interested in dealing with him, only to have pithy invective heaped on her head.

Just when she thought the day couldn't get any worse, her secretary relayed,

'Georgia Burton is in reception.'

Katrina felt her stomach twist at the announcement. It would be easy to insist Georgia make an appointment, with no advantage except to delay the confrontation.

'Show her in.' Nerves had her smoothing a hand over her hair and repairing her lipstick. She'd just tossed the capped tube into her drawer when a discreet knock at the door preceded Georgia's entrance.

The model looked a million dollars in a pale silk suit, an artfully draped scarf, stiletto heels, and perfectly applied make-up.

Katrina indicated one of three comfortable chairs. 'Please, take a seat.' In a calculated movement she checked her watch. 'I have to attend a scheduled meeting in ten minutes.'

'Darling, five minutes will do.' Georgia crossed to the plate-glass window and took a few valuable seconds to look out over the city before turning towards Katrina.

'Nicos and I have struck a deal.'

Don't let her get to you. 'Indeed?'

'I thought you'd be interested.'

'Why would you think that?'

'Doesn't it bother you that Nicos still continues to see me?'

'Should it?'

'Yes, considering you're an obstacle that prevents him being a father to his son.'

'An obstacle you intend to remove?'

'I'm glad you get the drift.'

'That this is a last-ditch effort on your part?' she queried with deadly softness. 'How long, Georgia, before due legal process forces the release of your son's DNA results?' Her gaze didn't falter as she mentally sharpened her claws. 'A day, hours, before your elaborate scheme falls apart?'

'Nikki is Nicos's son!'

'I'm sure you wish that were true.' Katrina aimed for the kill, and played the biggest gamble of her life. 'But it's not, is it?' Dear Lord, what if she was wrong?

Georgia's eyes narrowed. 'Two days ago Nicos was in Brisbane with me.'

'A meeting which took place in a lawyer's office.'

'Is that what he told you?'

'What if I told you I have a private detective's report tabling Nicos's every move?' She didn't, but Georgia wasn't to know that.

'Then, you have precise details of each liaison.'

Stay calm, Katrina bade silently. She's merely calling your bluff. Or was she? *Don't go there.*

Summoning icy control Katrina stood to her feet and crossed to the door. 'You'll have to excuse me.'

Georgia's features were composed, her voice dripping with pseudo sympathy. 'He may remain married to you, darling, but he'll always be mine.'

She swept out the door with the sort of smile that made Katrina want to smash something.

Déjà vu, she reflected grimly as she crossed back to her desk.

Nine months ago she'd stood in this office shattered beyond belief at the news Georgia was pregnant with Nicos's child.

Had she been wrong? Could Georgia have contrived evidence that, while appearing irrefutable, was in fact erroneous?

Nicos had asserted his innocence from the beginning. *What if he was right?*

There was nothing she could do, but wait for the DNA results to be released.

Lunch wasn't even an option, and by mid-afternoon she was punchy. Make that *very* punchy, she determined after taking a call from her wayward and very persistent stepbrother.

She couldn't even threaten to expose him to Chloe, for his mother was well aware of his habitual need for money and *why*. It was, Chloe had explained languidly, a phase. As far as Katrina was concerned, Enrique had long outgrown this *phase* and was several steps down the path to addiction.

It was five-thirty when she left the office, and she joined the commuter trail of bumper-to-bumper vehicles clogging the city's arterial routes leading to suburbs on all compass points.

Nicos's car was already in the garage when she parked the Boxster close by, and he was there in the lobby when she entered it.

Katrina threw him a fulminating glare as she bypassed him and made for the stairs. 'Don't even ask.' And she missed the way his eyebrow slanted with cynical bemusement as he viewed her ascending.

When she reached the landing she deftly removed one heeled pump, then the other, and by the time she reached the bedroom she'd unbuttoned her jacket, had loosened the camisole she wore beneath it, and was working on the zip fastening of her skirt.

A minute later she walked naked into the *en suite*, cast the spa-bath a covetous glance, longing to sink into the capacious tub and have the numerous jets work magic on her tense muscles...except she couldn't afford the luxury of unlimited time.

The shower beckoned, and she twisted the dial, adjusted the temperature, then stepped beneath the cascading water, collected the rose-scented soap and began lathering her skin.

She felt tired and emotionally wrung out and, dammit, she hurt in places she didn't even want to think about.

A slight sound alerted her attention, and she turned, gasping out loud as Nicos stepped naked into the shower stall with her.

'What in hell do you think you're doing?'

He took the soap from her nerveless fingers. 'I'd think it was obvious.'

'Oh, no, you don't,' Katrina said with a growl as he smoothed the soap over her shoulder. She made to grab it from him, and failed. 'Give me that!'

'Why don't you just relax?'

Relax? She was about as relaxed as a tightly coiled spring. *'Don't.'*

His hands were effecting a soothing massage at the edge of her neck, and she gave a silent groan that was part pleasure, part despair as his fingers eased out the kinks, then shifted down her back, inch by blissful inch, then they began working their way up again.

It felt so good, she forgot her anger, the tension of the day, and she simply closed her eyes and relaxed beneath his touch.

He soaped every inch of her skin, slowly, and she

sighed as his fingers trailed the contours of her breast, then travelled low over her hips.

'We don't have time for this.'

'Yes, we do.'

His fingers slid towards her navel, then slipped down to tease the soft curling hair at the apex of her thighs...and stroked with unerring expertise.

'We shouldn't arrive late.' She groaned as sensation began a slow spiral through her body.

'No,' Nicos murmured in agreement, shifting his hands to bring her close against him.

He lowered his mouth over hers, gently brushing his lips against her own, then he slid his tongue between her teeth and initiated a slow, sensual exploration that heated her blood and sent her pulse thudding to a quickened beat.

She slid her hands to his shoulders and clung as he deepened the kiss to something so incredibly erotic she lost track of time and place. There was just the two of them, and the magic that was theirs alone.

Nicos eased back from the brink of passion, softening his mouth as he trailed his lips over hers, pressing light kisses to each corner, the slightly swollen lower curve, before burying his mouth into the vulnerable hollow at the base of her neck.

How long did they remain like that? Five minutes? Ten? *More?*

Katrina felt wonderfully mellow, and filled with a lazy warmth that crept towards wanting more.

'We should get out of here,' she began to say tentatively, and felt his lips trail up to settle against her temple.

'Uh-huh.'

She leaned forward and closed the water dial while Nicos snagged a towel, handing it to her before catching up another for himself.

The temptation to linger was great. Even greater was the need to stay in and not venture from the bedroom at all.

'Later,' Nicos promised, his eyes dark with slumbering passion as he pressed a finger to her lips.

The art exhibition was held in a city gallery, featuring up-and-coming artists among whom two were gaining coveted acclaim.

Katrina wandered among the strategically placed paintings, and gravitated towards one that had caught her eye.

There was something in the use of colours that reminded her of Monet and the garden theme he so loved to depict on canvas. Beautifully framed, it reminded her of the French countryside with its fresh fields and flowers.

'Like it?'

'Yes, I do.' It would look perfect in her apartment. Or better yet, hanging on a wall in her office.

She moved on, aware Nicos had become caught up in conversation with a fellow business associate.

'Dear Katrina, we do seem to garner invitations to the same events.'

'Enrique.' She acknowledged. 'Why am I not surprised to see you here?'

'I have contacts, connections,' he relayed with a glib smile. 'Schmoozing is the name of the game, and I excel at working a room.'

'Alone?'

'Young, budding artists aren't Chloe's thing. Have you thought about my offer?'

'I don't need to think. The answer, as always, is the same.'

'Katrina,' Enrique chastised, shaking his head. 'I'm willing to trade information to your advantage.'

'No.'

'*No?*' He waited a beat. 'Aren't you in the least curious to hear some interesting facts about Georgia's love-child? Facts Nicos can substantiate?'

A cold hand clenched round her heart. 'That's old news.'

'It made good copy at the time.'

'Is there anything you won't do for money?' she demanded fiercely.

'I have an expensive habit, darling, which needs constant feeding.' His smile reminded her of a shark baring its teeth. 'It matters little whether the newspaper pays me, or you do.'

'Go to hell.'

'I take it that's a *no*?'

'A very definite and permanent refusal to your demands, now or at any time in the future,' Nicos said in a dangerously quiet voice. 'Take heed, Enrique. If you contact Katrina again, I'll have a restraining order served on you before you can blink.'

'You can't threaten me!'

Belligerence tempered with false bravado didn't augur well with a man of Nicos's calibre. 'I've stated facts.' His voice was hard, almost deadly with intent. 'It's your choice whether you comply or not.'

Enrique cast Katrina a look that was filled with animosity. 'You owe me. Kevin owes me.'

'Harassment is a punishable offence,' Nicos reminded him with chilling softness.

Enrique swore. 'I hope you both rot in hell.' He turned and began threading his way through the milling guests.

'Charming.'

Nicos inclined his head. 'Indeed.'

'I think I'll go check out some of the exhibits.'

He fell into step beside her, and they hadn't moved far when a guest signalled his attention. Katrina offered a polite greeting, then left the two men to talk.

'Something to drink, ma'am?'

Katrina smiled at the hovering waiter, and selected a flute of champagne from a proffered tray, then she browsed among the exhibits, returning to the painting she'd admired. It held a discreet sold sticker, and she felt a stab of disappointment, mentally cursing herself for not seeking out the gallery owner and negotiating a price.

'I think,' Nicos drawled as he rejoined her, 'we've provided sufficient patronage. Shall we leave?'

There were a few acquaintances present among the guests, and it took long minutes to observe the social niceties before they were able to escape the gallery.

'Hungry?'

She cast him a solemn glance as he eased the car out of its parking bay. 'Are you offering me food?'

'Did you manage lunch?'

She hadn't managed breakfast either, and had subsisted on fruit, a sandwich her secretary had sent out for, and coffee, tea and juice throughout the day.

Somehow finger food comprising canapés, miniature vol-au-vents and crackers with cheese proffered at the gallery were no substitute for a meal.

'Not as such,' she admitted, observing the short distance the car travelled before sliding to the kerb adjacent to a trendy pavement café in Double Bay.

The menu was a mix of exotic-sounding dishes, and she chose a prawn risotto with bruschetta, followed by black coffee. Nicos ordered the same, and they sipped iced mineral water as they waited for the food to arrive.

Katrina was supremely conscious of him, aware the fine clothes were merely the sophisticated trappings of a man whose heart moved to a primitive beat. It was evident in the way he held himself, his eyes reflecting an innate strength, a power that combined a dramatic mesh of elemental ruthlessness with indomitable will. Add latent sensuality, and it became something lethal, mesmeric.

Rarely had she seen him exert due force, or resort to anger. Except for last night. It had been like unleashing a tiger, and she shivered slightly at the memory.

'Cold?'

She'd worn elegant evening trousers, with a matching camisole and jacket, and the night was mild. 'No.'

A waiter presented their food, and they ate with leisurely ease, then lingered over coffee.

It was after eleven when Nicos garaged the car and they made their way indoors. The events of the past few days were beginning to have their effect, and all she wanted to do was remove her clothes and crawl into bed.

'Let me do that.'

Katrina shot him a startled glance as his fingers took care of the buttons on her jacket. The camisole came next, followed by the trousers, which he slid gently down over her hips, and she stepped out of them, then toed off her stiletto-heeled pumps.

She murmured in protest when his hands reached for her bra clip, and she stilled as he began easing free her bikini briefs.

'Nicos—'

He stilled anything further she might have said by placing a finger over her mouth, and she stood helplessly as he divested his own clothes.

In one fluid movement he placed an arm beneath her knees and carried her into bed with him.

'Now, where were we?'

His fingertips drifted to her waist, explored one hip, then trailed to settle at the apex between her thighs.

A sound that was part groan, half sigh, whispered from her lips, and her mouth parted beneath his own as he took her down a path towards sensual ecstasy.

Last night had been in anger, and there was a need

to make amends for the intensity of his emotions, the loss of control.

Tonight was for her, and he took it slowly, employing such incredible gentleness she was on the verge of tears when he slid into her.

Afterwards, he held her close, his lips buried in her hair as she drifted to sleep.

CHAPTER ELEVEN

Nicos had already left when Katrina entered the kitchen, and she popped bread into the toaster, poured coffee, then she balanced a cup and a plate, tucked the daily newspaper beneath her arm and opted to eat breakfast on the terrace.

The sun's warmth was enticing, the air still…a perfect spring morning. Tiny buds were beginning to emerge along the garden borders. Soon, multicoloured impatiens would burst into new life, and the lattice along the back wall would display a tapestry of multicoloured sweet peas.

Peace and tranquillity, Katrina mused. She bit into her toast, then sipped the hot, sweet black coffee as she skimmed the daily headlines.

Until she reached the gossip column.

Which prominent Sydney businessman, recently reconciled with his heiress wife, has been exonerated of fatherhood by DNA testing? The ploy by an ex-mistress to provide herself with a meal ticket has failed due to the success of medical science.

Nicos? Katrina's stomach twisted into a painful knot. Following Enrique's directive yesterday, the reference held too many coincidences for it not to be.

Dear heaven. She felt sickened as the implications began to sink in.

She looked blindly out over the landscape, not seeing the superb view, the terraced pool. Her mind was a kaleidoscope of remembered images.

The nine months between then and now disappeared in a flash. She felt the pain as if it were yesterday.

Georgia informing her she was pregnant with Nicos's child. Nicos's disavowal. Her own disbelief. The arguments. The chilling silences. Followed by Katrina's decision to leave.

In seeming slow motion she caught up her plate and cup, the newspaper, and carried them into the kitchen. With automatic movements she rinsed and stacked the dishwasher, then dressed for work.

She called her office, said she was delayed, and half an hour later she entered the elegant suite of offices Nicos occupied downtown.

Getting past reception took only the necessary time for the girl behind the desk to buzz his secretary, only to have her offer her personal regrets that Nicos was engaged in an important meeting.

'It's a matter of urgency.' Her urgency to discover the truth.

'I've been instructed not to disturb Mr Kasoulis under any circumstances.'

'I'll take the blame,' Katrina said coolly.

The boss, or the boss's wife? Each were irretrievably linked, and she sensed the secretary's dilemma.

'I'll tell him you're here,' his secretary conceded

after a few seconds' silence, and crossing to the desk she picked up the phone and made the call. Seconds later she replaced the handset. Her expression was carefully composed as she turned back to her boss's wife. 'I'll show you through to Mr Kasoulis's office. He'll join you in a few minutes.'

It was a large corner office, with magnificent views of Port Jackson harbour. Antique furniture, leather buttoned chairs, genuine oil paintings on the walls.

Katrina crossed to the tinted, floor-to-ceiling plate-glass window, and stood watching a passenger ferry as it headed towards the Manly terminal. A huge tanker lay anchored in the entrance, awaiting a tug-boat to guide it into a designated berth. A peaceful scene that was totally at variance with the turmoil seething beneath the surface of her control.

The almost silent click of the door closing caused her to turn, and she wore Nicos's raking appraisal as he closed the distance between them.

'What is it?'

Katrina felt the knot in her stomach tighten as he reached her side. Oh, hell, just cut to the chase. She slid the newspaper clipping from her jacket pocket, and handed it to him. 'Read this.'

He was good, she conceded. There was no change in his physical expression as he scanned the newsprint. Then he crunched it into a ball and tossed it in the direction of a waste-paper basket. 'For that, you pulled me out of a meeting?'

'I consider it important.'

Nicos cast her a long, level look that was impossible to read. 'Of such urgency it couldn't wait until this evening?'

'No.'

'You want me to confirm it?'

'Yes,' she stated simply.

'Let me guess,' Nicos began with marked indolence. 'Georgia confided in Enrique, who then sold the information to a newspaper contact?'

'*Yes*,' Katrina reiterated. Her eyes flashed with long withheld anger. 'Dammit, you could have told me yourself instead of leaving me to discover facts from a newspaper!'

'*When* would you have had me confide my intention to have Georgia provide tissue samples for DNA testing, Katrina?' His voice was pure silk. 'Should I have introduced it as idle conversation during the few social functions where we accidentally happened to attend at the same time? As Kevin lay dying in hospital? At his funeral?'

Katrina's gaze sharpened. 'You *knew* Kevin had redrawn his will, incorporating the condition stipulating my control of Macbride.' The anger began to build, gaining momentum. 'So you waited. Both of you making the decision to take advantage of a bad situation.'

'Yes.'

Her eyes sparked green fire. 'You didn't have that right!'

'The least I could do for him, and you, was to allow him your total focus, unclouded by other issues which could be resolved—'

'At a later date.' A cold hand closed around her heart. 'And if Kevin's health hadn't been in jeopardy?'

His gaze was hard, inflexible, almost dangerous. 'You doubt I would have told you?'

She couldn't be sure. She wanted to be. Desperately, with all her heart.

Nicos read the momentary indecision, the aching intensity of her emotions. Yet still he waited.

'Do you know what I went through when Georgia confronted me with her pregnancy and named you as the father of her unborn child?' she demanded.

'At the time, I distinctly recall stating my relationship with Georgia was over long before I met you.'

She'd chosen not to believe him. 'You have to admit the evidence seemed weighted against you.' Dear heaven, the barbs, the innuendo had been very cleverly orchestrated. 'Georgia provided dates, places, that coincided with your absence.'

'Even given there was any truth in it, do you think I would have been sufficiently foolish not to take precautions against a possible pregnancy?' he continued relentlessly.

'Prophylactic protection has been known to break.'

Nicos wanted to wring her slender neck. 'I gave you my word. It should have been enough.'

Kevin had believed in him. Why hadn't she?

Because Georgia had pressed all the right buttons, she perceived silently. Shock, disbelief, anger had done the rest.

Anger flared. 'What did you expect, Nicos? That

I'd turn a blind eye? Dammit, my heart felt as if it had been ripped from my body!'

'Did you spare a thought for my reaction?' His voice dropped to a dangerous softness. 'Have you tried beating your head against a brick wall, yet make no impression?'

She was temporarily bereft of speech.

'Do you know how long it took for me to get proof of my innocence? How many legal battles I fought to have Georgia submit to DNA testing during her pregnancy? And failed?' His features assumed an angry mask. 'How the legal system forced me to wait until the child was born, *and* go through the process of a court order to have DNA tissue testing carried out on the child?'

'Just *how long* have you known the result of the DNA test?' she demanded.

'Since late yesterday afternoon.'

He thrust his fists into his trouser pockets in an attempt at control. 'Georgia's intention was to latch onto me for child support, and acquire a meal ticket for life. She didn't care who got in the way. Or who she hurt.' His eyes were hard, his expression inflexible. 'It seems the father of the child is a charming playboy living far beyond his means. They set up the scenario together.'

Her expressive features conveyed more than mere words, unaware he read every emotion.

'You doubt I would leave any stone unturned?' he queried hardily.

Katrina stood silent for several seemingly long seconds.

'I have copies of court documents, reports from private detectives, and now the DNA result,' Nicos explained.

Nine months of anguish, broken dreams, lonely nights. They had each experienced their own individual hell, caused by a woman whose wicked inability to let go of an ex-lover had damaged their lives and had almost wrecked their marriage.

To think how close Georgia came to achieving her goal... It made Katrina shudder to even contemplate it.

'I owe you an apology.' Her voice was stiff, the words almost disjointed.

His gaze held hers. 'Are you offering one?'

A whole gamut of emotions crowded for release. 'Yes, dammit!' Oh, hell, she wouldn't cry. That would be the final humiliation. Her chin tilted as she fought for control. 'You're right. Here, now, isn't the time or place for this.'

She turned away from him and took two steps towards the door, only to have a hand close over her arm as he pulled her back towards him.

'Oh, no,' Nicos said with lethal softness. 'You aren't going to walk away this time.'

Her eyes shimmered with unshed tears. 'What do you want?'

Her voice broke, and it almost undid him.

'You hold me to blame for using the terms of Kevin's will?' he demanded quietly. 'Taking the opportunity to repair what Georgia had torn apart?' He waited a few seconds, then pursued her, saying, 'Proving to you that what we shared was too special to cast aside?' He released her arm and thrust hands into his trouser pockets so as not to catch hold of her shoulders and shake her.

'I needed for you to *see*, to *feel* you're the only woman in my life. Each time we came together, you had to *know* it was an act of love. Not just physical sex to scratch an itch.'

Dear God, she had known. Deep down in a sub-conscious level, there had been recognition. She should have listened to her instincts, instead of allowing Georgia's vicious innuendo to take root.

'Except once,' Nicos revealed darkly. 'When I hauled you back from the hotel.' He smote a fist into the palm of his hand, and the explosive sound echoed starkly round the room. 'I was so angry at yet another legal delay; then to arrive home and discover you gone... I was so close, yet still not close enough to a resolution. To have you openly defy me attacked the barriers of my control.' He lifted a hand and pushed fingers through his hair. 'I lost it. And shocked you.'

'No, you overwhelmed me,' Katrina corrected. '*You* were always the one in control of your emotions. To have you display such a degree of unleashed passion was exciting. Mind-blowing,' she added. There was nothing left. Not even pride. 'I loved you so much.' It was all she had. Words. Yet they came from the depths of her soul.

Something moved in his eyes, fleetingly, then it was gone. He lifted a hand and brushed his knuckles over her cheek. 'And now?'

'It never changed,' she admitted simply.

'Thank you.' He knew what it cost her to say it.

He touched the tip of his thumb to her lips, felt them quiver, and offered a faint smile. 'Was that so hard?'

'Yes.'

Such honesty, so hard-won. His fingers slid down her throat, caressed the hollow there, then slipped to cup her nape.

Her mouth was soft, tremulous beneath his own, and he savoured it gently, then took her deep, with such passionate intensity there could be no room for doubt.

He felt the breath sigh from her throat, caught it, and pulled her in against him until the softness of her body melded to the hardness of his own.

His hand slid down her back, shaped the firm buttocks, then paused on her thigh, aware of its line, before shifting beneath her skirt.

The heat of her flesh drove him almost to the edge, and he had no other thought but to divest her clothes, his own, and ravish her here, now, uncaring of time or place.

He explored the moistness, sent her up and over, then caressed with an expertise that drove her wild.

It was almost more than she could bear, and her fingers tore at the buttons on his shirt, found the skin she so desperately sought, and moved lower in a feverish craving to touch him as he was stroking her. Until he was past need, beyond hunger.

Dear heaven, it wasn't enough. Not nearly enough.

His mouth left hers, trailed the slim column of her neck, then grazed her throat, nibbling the swollen softness of her lower lip before plundering at will.

Katrina became lost, so caught up with him, she was hardly aware he had dragged his mouth from hers until she registered the insistent buzz of the in-house phone.

'Kasoulis.' His voice was hard, inflexible, and she swayed slightly, then moved back a step.

Only to have him circle her wrist and hold her still.

His eyes never left hers, and she felt her own widen as she took in his dishevelled clothes, the state of her usually immaculate business suit.

'Reschedule, please. Tomorrow afternoon.'

Katrina could imagine his secretary's response.

'I don't give a damn what excuse you offer.'

Nicos listened, then cut in, 'The deal is more important to them than it is to me. They'll concede.' He cut the connection.

Katrina tried for calm, and failed miserably. 'I should go.'

'We are.' He brushed light fingers over her breasts, lingered, then reluctantly tended to the buttons on her blouse.

With deft movements he redid his own buttons, tucked his shirt back into his trousers, and straightened his tie.

His mouth curved into a lazy smile. 'Somewhere with no interruptions.'

'But you have an important meeting—'

'I just cancelled.'

A witching glimmer of humour danced in her eyes. 'So you did.'

He kissed her briefly, a swift, evocative gesture that didn't begin to satisfy.

Katrina watched as Nicos negotiated the traffic, aware of him to a heightened degree. His male scent, the faint tang of his cologne.

He possessed an elemental sexuality that stirred her senses to fever pitch. Primitive, raw, and wholly mesmeric, it had the power to turn her into a willing wanton woman, shameless, libidinous, and totally *his*.

'A hotel?'

'You want to shock Sofia and Andre?'

She shot him a mischievous smile. 'I guess not.'

Katrina slid from the passenger seat as Nicos handed the car over to a porter, and she entered the spacious lobby, admired a magnificent floral arrangement as Nicos checked in, then entered the lift at his side.

Could the other occupants sense the shimmering passion? It was all she could do not to reach out and touch him.

There were words she longed to say, but they could wait. What they wanted, needed, from each other, could not.

Nicos drew her into the suite, fixed the do-not-disturb sign, locked the door, then drew her into his arms.

His mouth closed over hers with a hunger she met and matched, their hands busy as they discarded each layer of clothing, until there was the warmth and intimacy of skin on skin.

Heat and passion, desire and hunger. Wild ravaging need.

Now.

It was a silent language two lovers shared, and a groan escaped her throat as he lifted her high, then slid into her with one powerful thrust, his hands caging her hips.

Katrina flung back her head, exultant in his possession, and she simply held on as he captured her breast, teasing the tender peak until she cried out for mercy. Only to have him ravish its twin.

Her hands slid to his shoulders, then moved up to hold fast his head as she brought it to her own in a kiss that mirrored the sexual act itself.

It was a turbulent coupling, and she gasped as he took her deep, only to withdraw and take her again, long slow movements to maximise her pleasure.

She sensed the moment he was at the brink of losing control, and she joined him as they tipped over the edge, his husky groan mingling with her own in a climax that left them both shuddering their release.

He held her close, nuzzling the sensitive skin at the edge of her neck until the raggedness of their breathing slowed and evened out.

Then he carried her into the bathroom, filled the

spa-bath, and lifted her into the pulsating water before retreating to the bar fridge for champagne.

Katrina sipped the chilled contents of her flute as he stepped in to sit facing her.

'*Salute.*' He touched the rim of her flute with his own, and her lips parted in a winsome smile.

She felt almost in awe of the entire gamut of emotions invading her senses. There was love, its strength and tenure overwhelming. An intense awareness there could be no one else, ever, capable of taking his place in her heart.

It was a knowledge imprinted in her soul. Inviolate.

Nicos lifted a hand and trailed light fingers across her cheek, watched her eyes dilate as he traced the outline of her generous mouth.

Her lips parted, soft and slightly swollen beneath his touch.

'Thank you.'

One eyebrow lifted slightly. 'For what, precisely?'

Her eyes were the darkest green, and incredibly eloquent. '*You,*' she said simply. His tenacity, everything that made him the man he was. To consider, even for a moment, that he might have let her walk away filled her with pain.

'You're mine,' Nicos said gently. 'No other woman comes close to you.'

It hurt unbearably that she had doubted him. Yet the purported facts had been damning, at the time his denial beyond proof. And Georgia had been very convincing. Such incredible lengths Nicos's former mistress had gone to destroy a marriage.

A faint shiver slithered down her spine. That Georgia had almost succeeded—

'Don't go there.'

He read her so well. Too well, she attested silently.

Nicos caught her close and savoured the sweet curve of her shoulder. His hands soothed, brushing lightly over water-slicked skin, pausing to render supplication to vulnerable pleasure pulses before drifting low in an evocative trail that stirred her senses anew.

A soft sigh left her lips as his fingers caressed the sensitised nub, taking her high with a skilled ease that left her breathless.

'Nicos.' His name was both plea and protest.

'Hmm?' His voice was a teasing murmur at her temple.

'If you plan taking this further, I should tell you I skipped lunch.'

His husky laughter was almost her undoing. 'I thought I had your undivided attention.'

Katrina placed her lips against his in a brief teasing kiss. 'You do.' Believe me, you do, she added silently.

He rose to his feet in one fluid movement, lifted her effortlessly onto the tiled floor, then wrapped a towel round her slim form before fixing another at his hips.

'Let's go check out room service.'

It was later, after a leisurely meal and what remained of the champagne, that Katrina caught hold of his hand and pulled him towards her.

'Do you have plans for this evening?'

He gave a faint smile. 'We could go home.'

The word had a nice sound to it. 'Hmm,' she teased, pretending to consider their choices. 'Or we could get dressed.' She fingered his complimentary towelling robe, one of which she also wore. 'And take in a nightclub.'

So she wanted to play. He was willing to join in the game. 'Or a movie.'

Katrina traced a finger down the deep V of his robe. 'It would be a shame to waste the suite.'

He stood still, content to let her have control, for now. 'A shame.'

She teased the dark hairs arrowing down to his waist. 'Do we have any wine?'

'Red, or white?'

Her faint smile held a wicked tinge. 'It doesn't matter.'

'Want me to check?'

Her fingers were busy, and far too close to a vulnerable part of his anatomy.

'Uh-huh.'

Nicos moved a few paces, retrieved a small bottle of wine, popped the cork, part-filled two goblets and handed her one.

Katrina dipped a forefinger into the light-coloured liquid, traced a pattern along the edge of his collar bone, then she leaned forward and slowly followed the same path with her tongue.

With one hand she undid the tie fastening his robe and pushed it off one shoulder, then the other, letting it fall to the floor in a heap.

His eyes were dark, and she saw the pulse leap at his throat as she circled one male nipple.

Minutes later his breath hissed through his teeth, and firm fingers closed over her wrist, stilling the evocative trail. 'Dear God,' he ground out. 'Are you done?'

She tilted her head, and her lips curved into a provocative smile. 'Had enough?'

A muscle clenched at the edge of his jaw. 'Be warned, I intend to reciprocate.'

A light laugh escaped her throat. 'I'm counting on it.'

Later, much later, it was she who groaned out loud. She who pleaded, then begged as he took her on a mercilessly provocative journey that explored the senses until she shattered, fragmenting into a thousand, exquisite pieces.

Katrina lay supine, seriously doubting her ability to move. Even lifting a hand seemed to require too much effort. She was barely aware when Nicos pulled up the bed covers, and drew her in close against him.

She slept, waking to the light brush of Nicos's fingers as he traced a line along the edge of her waist to her hip, then her thigh. His lips teased the soft hollow at the base of her throat, and she moved close to nuzzle his chest.

It was a wonderful way to begin the day. Slow, lazy seduction, and equally slow sex.

Lovemaking, she qualified, glorying in the feel and the taste of him.

Afterwards they hit the shower together, then

dressed, they ordered in breakfast and ate it out on the terrace, watching the city come alive as ferries crossed the harbour and road traffic began to build.

A new day, Katrina mused as she sipped the aromatic coffee. The sky was a clear blue, with hardly a cloud in sight, and the sun lent the promise of warmth.

There was a sense of timelessness, and a need to encapsulate the moment and store it somewhere safe.

Nicos studied her profile, the fine bone structure. She possessed a beauty of soul and spirit, an intrinsic quality that was uncontrived.

He felt his body harden remembering the degree of intimacy they'd shared. Two minds so finely attuned, he knew her thoughts, her innermost secrets.

Katrina's skin prickled, and she turned slightly, met his gaze, and felt her insides begin to melt at what she saw in those dark depths.

'Time to go,' she said gently as she rose to her feet and offered him her hand.

Together they took the lift down to reception and collected the car. Ten minutes later Nicos double-parked outside the towering steel and glass structure which housed the corporate offices of Macbride.

Katrina kissed her fingers and touched them briefly to his lips. 'Until tonight.'

He watched her disappear through the revolving glass doors, then he eased the car into the flow of traffic.

There was a place in the Greek Islands where the sun kissed the translucent waters, vines grew on the gentle slopes, and white-washed villas dotted the hill-side. He had an urge to take her there, to relax and enjoy the simple pleasures of life for a while. He'd have his secretary make the arrangements.

Within minutes of reaching his office he picked up the phone, issued specific instructions, and got on with the day.

Across town Katrina viewed the rectangular-shaped package the courier had just delivered, and removed the protective wrapping to reveal the painting she had admired at the art gallery.

She picked up the phone, dialled Nicos's number, and responded as soon as he answered.

'Thank you. It's beautiful.'

'My pleasure.'

His voice was warm, and sent tingles down her spine.

Minutes later there was another delivery, and she opened the slender florist box to discover a single long-stemmed red rose nestling in a swathe of tissue. The card read, '*Katrina, agape mou. Nicos.*'

My love. She lifted the rose to her cheek, savoured the velvety texture on her skin, then gently inhaled the delicate perfume.

Katrina had a plan of her own, and she implemented the arrangements, rang Siobhan with the invitation, then sank back into her chair with a warm smile.

'*A private dinner,*' Katrina declared as she rose from the bed next morning. 'In celebration,' she added, teasing gently, 'We get to dress up, for each other.'

'I gather this is something special?' Nicos queried as he joined her in the shower, and caught her nod in assent.

And it was. Very special. Her gift to him.

Had he guessed? she mused as she led him out into the gardens just before dusk. There, beneath the spreading branches of a beautiful jacaranda, stood a celebrant with Siobhan at his side.

'A reaffirmation of our wedding vows.'

Nicos drew her into his arms, settled his mouth over hers in a kiss that lasted long and took her breath away.

'You get to do that *after* the ceremony,' the celebrant teased gently.

'Count on it.'

Siobhan brushed a tear away as the celebrant intoned the words Katrina had requested. With joy for her daughter's newfound happiness, and the man who so obviously cherished her.

The meal Katrina had Marie prepare was a simple repast served in the candle-lit dining room. Chilled champagne and a single-tiered miniature wedding cake added an unexpected touch.

Afterwards Nicos drew Katrina into the study and slid a diamond-studded ring onto her finger.

'Eternity. Ours,' he said gently, watching her beautiful eyes coalesce with emotion. 'There's just one other thing.' He unlocked a desk drawer and handed her a document. 'Read it.'

Legalese, gifting her the one-third share bequest in Macbride originally assigned to him by Kevin Macbride.

'It was always yours,' Nicos relayed quietly. 'Now it's official.'

Words momentarily failed her, and she dashed the sudden tears that sprang to her eyes. 'I love you.' Tremulously spoken words that came straight from the heart. 'It never stopped.'

Nicos lifted both hands and gently cupped her face. 'I know.' He kissed her with lingering passion, then carried her upstairs to bed.

CHAPTER TWELVE

KATRINA repositioned herself on the low-set lounger and let the warm Aegean sun caress her bikini-clad body. Dark lenses protected her eyes, and she tipped the large straw hat over her face.

It had taken Nicos a few phone calls to delegate, book a flight to Athens, and organise hire of this elegant cruiser.

They'd been here a week. Lovely lazy days and long nights filled with lovemaking. Idyllic, she thought as she closed her eyes and let her mind drift.

All the doubts and turmoil, the insecurities, had vanished. A trial by fire, she reflected, wincing slightly as Georgia's spiteful image sprang vividly to mind.

'Don't,' Nicos cautioned gently. He was so keenly attuned to her that he sensed the slight tension evident, divined and sought to alleviate it as he brushed the pads of his fingers across her midriff in a soothing gesture.

Her skin was a light honey-gold, its texture silky smooth beneath his touch, and he took pleasure in the caress as he explored the line of Lycra stretching low across her hips.

The slight hitch in her breathing brought forth a faint smile, and he traced lower, witnessed the way her stomach muscles tightened, then he leaned towards her and bestowed a kiss on her navel.

'You're in danger of shocking the natives,' Katrina said in a husky drawl, and heard his soft laughter.

'There's not a soul in sight.'

'Binoculars, paparazzi and long-range-zoom camera lenses,' she reminded him indolently, not wanting to move.

He had the touch, the skill, that took her from warmth to heat in a few seconds flat. Desire and passion followed in equal time.

'Want to take this down below?'

A soft chuckle of laughter emerged from her throat, and she lifted a hand, tilted her hat so she could look at him. 'Are you serious?'

His answering grin held a wolfish quality. 'You're not?'

She pretended to consider her options. 'I guess I could be persuaded.' Remembering just how good he was at persuasion had her heartbeat moving up a notch.

His fingers pressed a vulnerable nub, so lightly she almost groaned in need of more.

'If you need to think about it...'

A hand snaked out and managed a grip onto his chest hair, tightened a little. 'Don't toy with me.'

Her husky growl was quickly silenced as his mouth took possession of hers in a kiss that promised flagrant seduction.

When he lifted his head she ran the edge of her

tongue over the slightly swollen contours of her mouth.

'Well, then. That settles it.' She lifted a hand and pressed fingers to his lips, felt them move in a gentle caress, then she rose to her feet in a single, fluid movement, tugging him upright.

The cruiser was large, the galley and bedroom spacious.

Nicos pulled her in close and rested his cheek against her head.

He took it slowly. They had all the time in the world, and he instigated a leisurely tasting, savouring each shudder, each hitch of her breath.

She was *his*. The most important thing in his life. Always had been, even when they'd been apart. There could never be anyone else to take her place in his heart.

He said the words, in soft, guttural Greek, then in English, and she felt the moisture well in her eyes at the depth of emotion evident.

She captured his head, let her hands slide to frame his face, searched his beloved features, and saw what she knew in her heart, the depths of her soul. The unconditional love of a man for one woman. Beyond boundaries, forever true. It was an infinitely precious gift. One she would treasure for the rest of her life.

'Promise me something,' Katrina began to say gently, and saw his smile.

'You have to ask?'

'Let's work at making every day special.'

'That's a given.'

'There's just one more thing.' She reached up and kissed him, a fleeting touch. 'You have my love, my trust.' Her mouth shook a little. 'Always.'

'As you have mine, *agape mou*,' he whispered softly, and proceeded to show her a depth of passion that surpassed anything they'd previously shared.

CALL THE ONES YOU LOVE OVER THE HOLIDAYS!

Save $25 off future book purchases when you buy any four Harlequin® or Silhouette® books in October, November and December 2001,

PLUS

receive a phone card good for 15 minutes of long-distance calls to anyone you want in North America!

WHAT AN INCREDIBLE DEAL!

Just fill out this form and attach 4 proofs of purchase (cash register receipts) from October, November and December 2001 books, and Harlequin Books will send you a coupon booklet worth a total savings of $25 off future purchases of Harlequin® and Silhouette® books, AND a 15-minute phone card to call the ones you love, anywhere in North America.

Please send this form, along with your cash register receipts as proofs of purchase, to:
In the USA: Harlequin Books, P.O. Box 9057, Buffalo, NY 14269-9057
In Canada: Harlequin Books, P.O. Box 622, Fort Erie, Ontario L2A 5X3
Cash register receipts must be dated no later than December 31, 2001.
Limit of 1 coupon booklet and phone card per household.
Please allow 4-6 weeks for delivery.

I accept your offer! Enclosed are 4 proofs of purchase. Please send me my coupon booklet and a 15-minute phone card:

Name: _____

Address: _____ City: _____

State/Prov.: _____ Zip/Postal Code: _____

Account Number (if available): _____

---

097 KJB DAGL
PHQ4013

If you enjoyed what you just read,
then we've got an offer you can't resist!

Take 2 bestselling love stories FREE!

Plus get a FREE surprise gift!

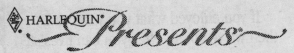

HARLEQUIN *Presents*

The world's bestselling romance series. Seduction and passion guaranteed!

Pick up a Harlequin Presents® novel and you will enter a world of spine-tingling passion and provocative, tantalizing romance!

Join us in 2002 for an exciting selection of titles from all your favorite authors:

Red Hot Revenge
COLE CAMERON'S REVENGE #2223, January
by Sandra Marton

Secret Passions
A truly thrilling new duet
THE SECRET VENGEANCE #2236, March
THE SECRET LOVE CHILD #2242, April
by Miranda Lee

A Mediterranean Marriage
THE BELLINI BRIDE #2224, January
by Michelle Reid
and
THE ITALIAN'S WIFE #2235, March
by Lynne Graham

An upbeat, contemporary story
THE CITY-GIRL BRIDE #2229, February
by Penny Jordan

An involving and dramatic read
A RICH MAN'S TOUCH #2230, February
by Anne Mather

On sale in the New Year
Available wherever Harlequin Books are sold.

HARLEQUIN®
Makes any time special®

Visit us at www.eHarlequin.com

HPDECPRE

Pick up a Harlequin Presents® novel and enter a world of spine-tingling passion and provocative, tantalizing romance!

Join us in December for two sexy Italian heroes from two of your favorite authors:

RAFAELLO'S MISTRESS
by Lynne Graham
#2217

THE ITALIAN'S RUNAWAY BRIDE
by Jacqueline Baird
#2219

HARLEQUIN *Presents*

The world's bestselling romance series.

Seduction and passion guaranteed.

Available wherever Harlequin books are sold.

Visit us at www.eHarlequin.com
HPITAL